DC COMIC[illegible]
SUPER[illegible] HEROES

[illegible]ou Ch[illegible]ose Stories →

BATMAN™

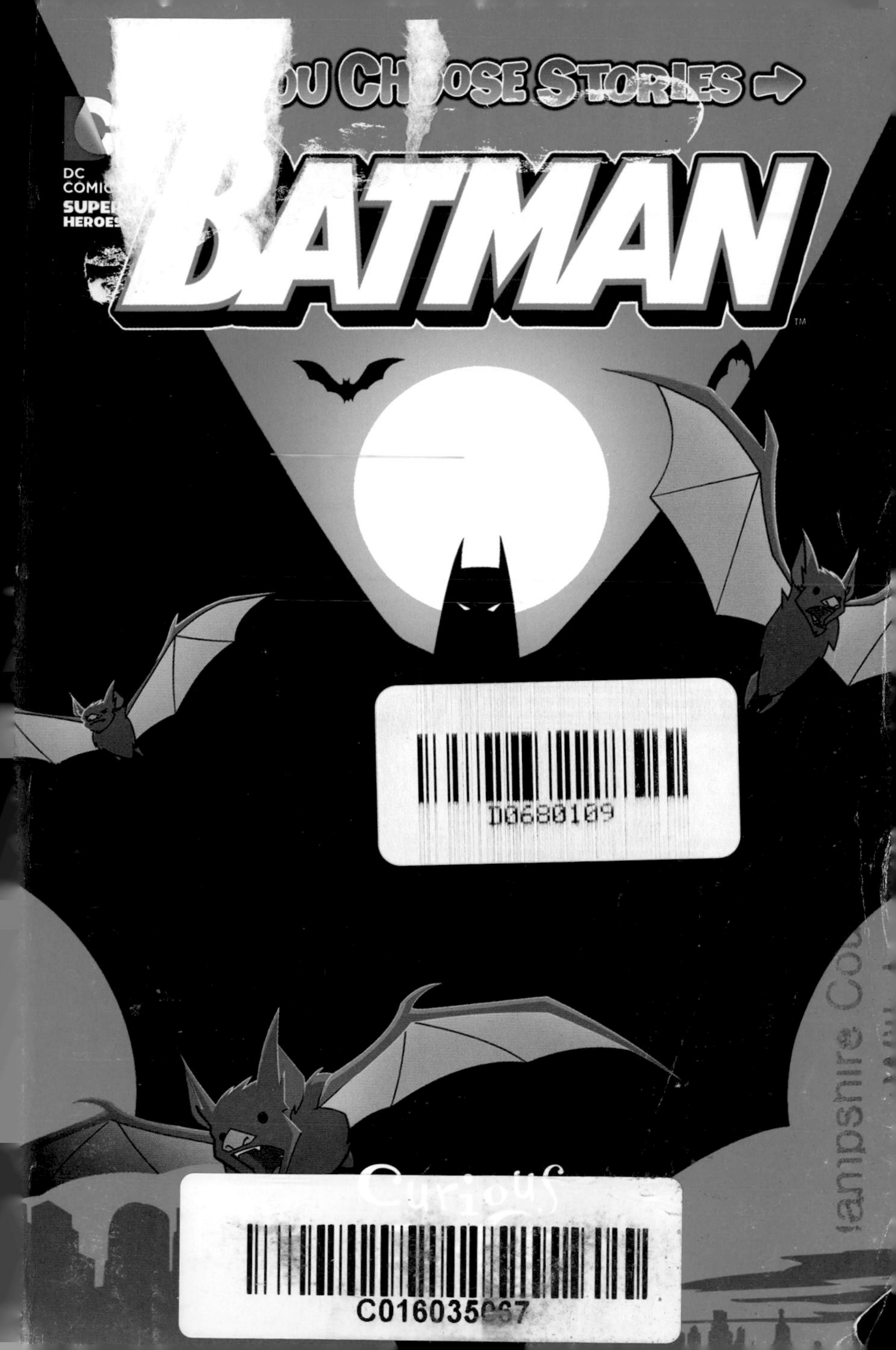

First published in this format in 2015 by Curious Fox,
an imprint of Capstone Global Library Limited, 7 Pilgrim
Street, London, EC4V 6LB – Registered company number:
6695582

www.curious-fox.com

CAPG34669

Printed and bound in China.

ISBN 978 1 782 02258 9
19 18 17 16 15
10 9 8 7 6 5 4 3 2 1

A CIP catalogue record for this book is available
from the British Library.

You CHOOSE STORIES

DC COMICS™
SUPER
HEROES

BATMAN™

SEED BANK HEIST

Batman created by Bob Kane

written by
J.E. Bright

illustrated by
Ethen Beavers

YOU CHOOSE STORIES

BATMAN

™

Poison Ivy has taken over a seed bank filled with the world's most historical and priceless plant seeds. Only YOU can help the Dark Knight stop this flower felon and her seed bank heist!

Follow the directions at the bottom of each page. The choices YOU make will change the outcome of the story. After you finish one path, go back and read the others for more Batman adventures!

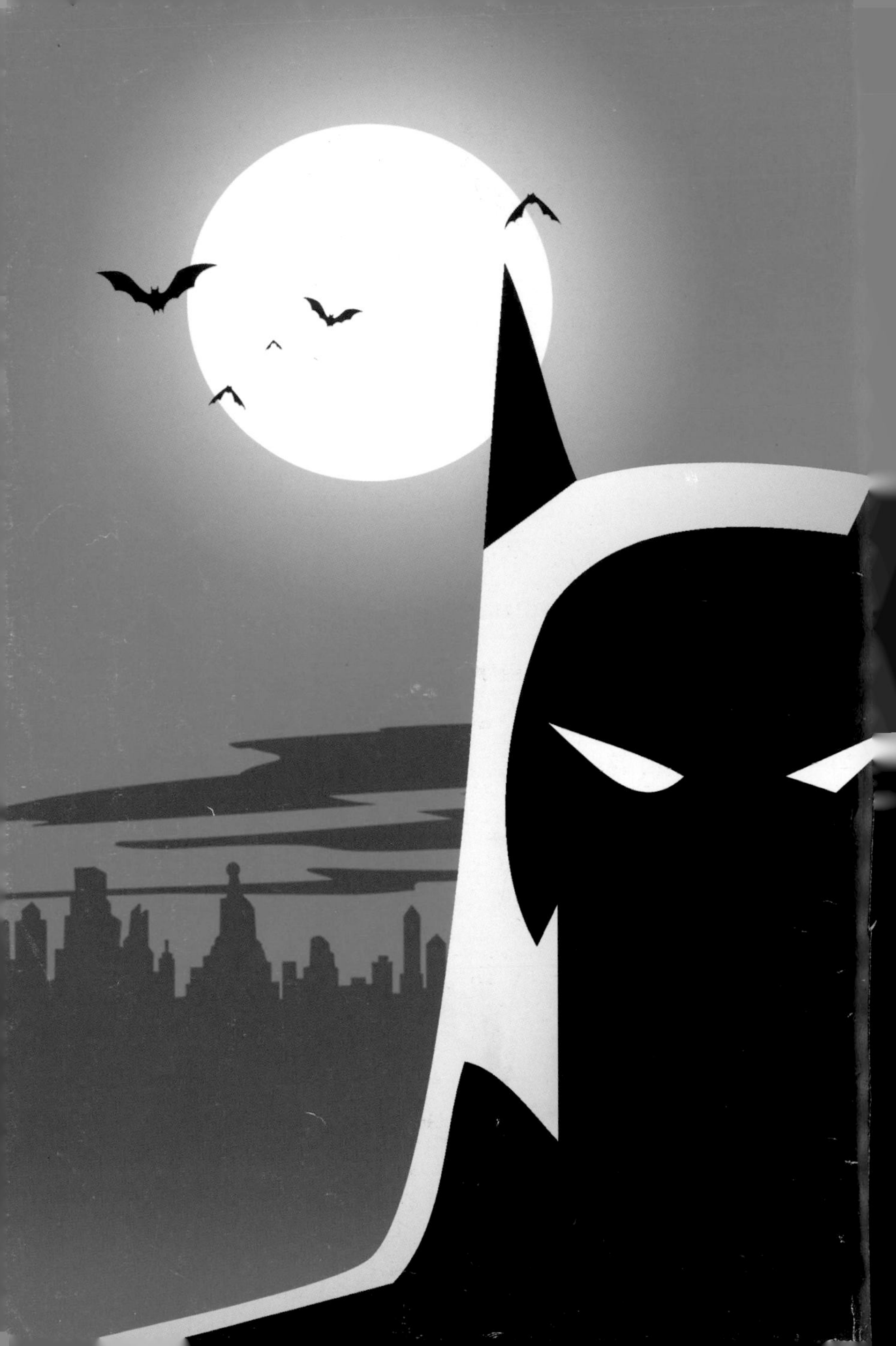

Dawn blooms on the dark horizon of downtown Gotham City.

After a night patrolling the violent streets, Batman heads towards Wayne Manor on his Batcycle. He scowls as he spots the Bat-Signal splashing on to bruise-coloured clouds. "Fine," he grumbles, turning his motorcycle back to Police Headquarters. "One last task before sleep."

Commissioner Gordon nods when Batman appears on the roof. He looks as weary as Batman feels. "There you are," says Gordon. "I wouldn't bother you so early if this wasn't important. There's been an escape from Arkham Asylum."

Turn the page.

"You need to beef up security there," says Batman.

"It's already the most high-tech prison in the world," replies Gordon.

Batman crosses his muscular arms. "Who got away this time?"

"Pamela Isley," Gordon answers. "Our flowery friend."

"Poison Ivy is no friend of ours," growls Batman. "She's a toxic villain who cares more about plants than humanity. Wasn't she kept free of vegetation for her to control?"

Commissioner Gordon checks his notes. "Security guard Aaron Cash informed us that Isley used moss. A spore entered her cell through a cracked water pipe. She made the moss grow giant roots, which split the walls."

"Any reports where she's headed?" the Dark Knight asks.

"We've gotten word she's on her way to the Giordano Botanical Gardens," replies Gordon.

Batman shakes his head. "This is not shaping up to be a good morning. Poison Ivy is too powerful in the gardens. She's literally a force of nature there."

The super hero jumps on the rooftop edge. "She'll get there before me," says Batman. "Have a strike force on standby."

As Batman swings down the fire escape to his Batcycle, he opens a map of Gotham City on his communicator. The image hovers in view through his goggles. "Burnley District," says Batman, and the map centres on northern Gotham. Arkham Island is far west, close to Giordano Gardens. The Police Department is in Old Gotham, the southern corner of the city.

Batman revs the Batcycle into motion. The gardens are forty-five minutes away … for a normal car following traffic laws. He can make it in fifteen, but that's too much time for Poison Ivy to wreak havoc.

Perhaps the new quantum booster on the Batcycle will close the gap.

Turn the page.

"Maximum speed," Batman commands.

Nine minutes later, the Batcycle skids to a halt, tires smoking. The parking lot of the Giordano Botanical Gardens is dotted with old maple and oak trees. Batman eyes them suspiciously. Every plant is a potential weapon.

A tall stone wall surrounds the garden complex. Batman leaves the Batcycle in defensive camouflage mode.

As he approaches the ticket booth, four people run out screaming. They're wearing matching green shirts with STAFF sewn in bold letters over the chest.

Batman catches a young man by the wrist. "Where is she?" he asks. "Poison Ivy."

The garden worker gasps, "Batman!" He pants as his co-workers scurry away. "I saw her ... on the great lawn. Towards the ... flower beds. All the plants were going crazy. She won't harm my roses, will she? They're delicate right now, blooming –"

"She'd die before hurting a rose," Batman assures the gardener. "It's the rest of Gotham City I'm worried about. Get to safety yourself."

Batman sprints down the park's main strip between a line of towering elms. Plants tremble and shimmy around him, awakened by Ivy's presence.

"Giordano Gardens data," he requests from his Batcomputer.

"Giordano Botanical Gardens is a horticultural park and research centre," the Batcomputer relays. "Specializing in conservation of endangered flora, with a world-renowned habitat for carnivorous plants –"

"Specs only," says Batman. He hurdles a bench and races on to a wide, rolling lawn, running towards the splashes of colour from the bushy flowerbeds on the other side.

Turn to page 13.

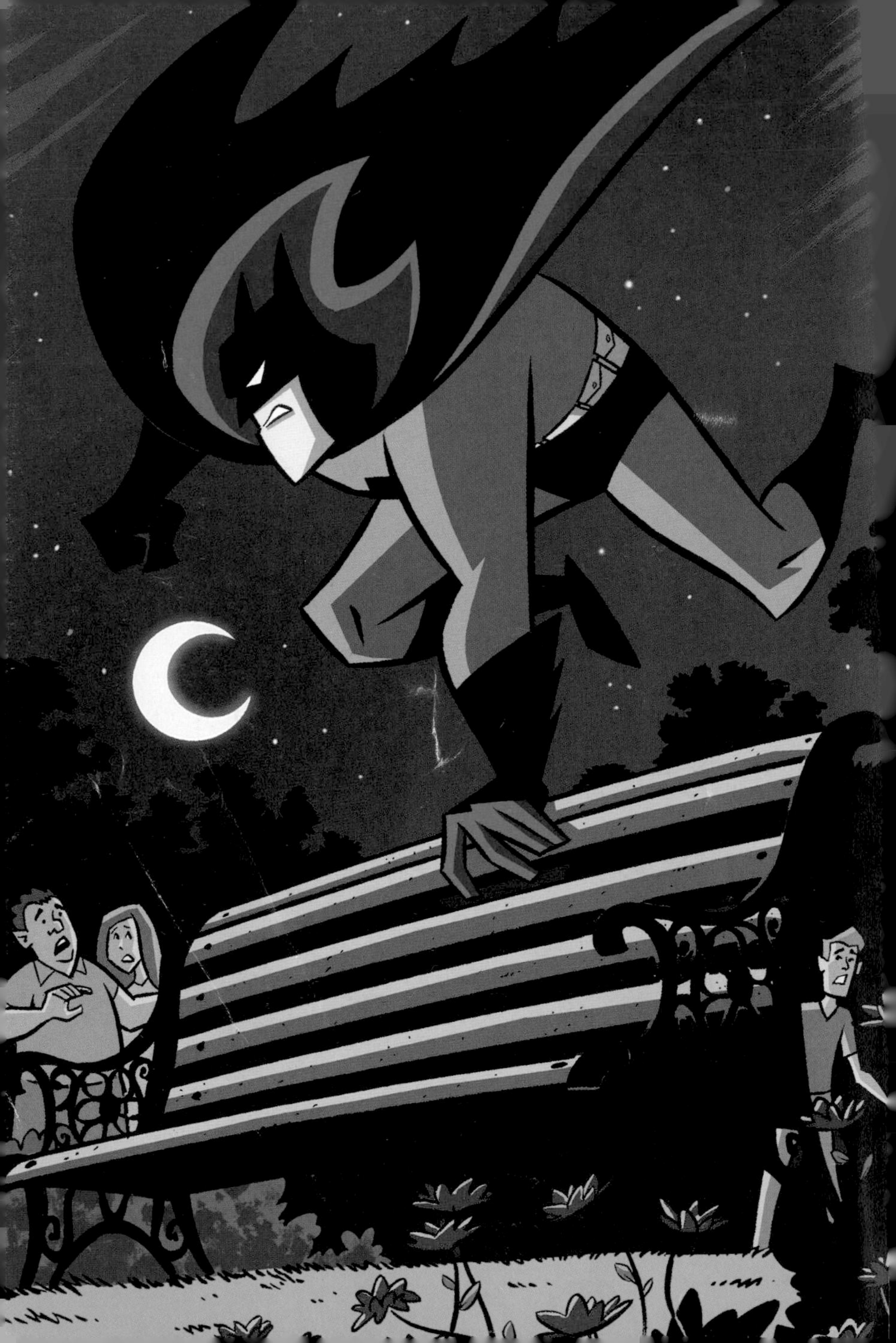

"Area: ninety acres total," the Batcomputer says. "Thirty-two acres outdoor garden. Forty-five acres forest, including a pine tree grove. Two bodies of water, a spring-fed lake and lily pond. The grounds and the Greenhouse Conservatory contain fifty thousand living plants, and more than five million species. The Greenhouse Conservatory is a classical glass structure, eighty-five thousand square feet in dimension –"

"How are non-living species stored?" asks Batman. He hurries towards a sign where three paths branch off into the flowerbeds.

"Millions are preserved as DNA samples in deep freeze," answers the Batcomputer. "In addition, the Wayne Seed Bank stores seeds in a chamber designed to withstand catastrophe."

As Bruce Wayne, majority owner of Wayne Enterprises, he signed a grant to fund the vault. It's crucial to protect the planet's biodiversity and food sources.

"That's what Ivy's after," says Batman. "She's robbing the seed bank!"

Turn the page.

He pauses at the edge of the flower garden.

Blossoms on the bushes, low trees, and stem beds flutter feverishly. Coral pink azaleas and red rhododendrons scintillate, spellbinding and alarming. Asters, mums and pansies shine and shimmer with dreamlike, deep shades of all colours of the rainbow.

The turmoil in the flowers can only mean one thing.

"Poison Ivy is near," mutters Batman.

Turn to page 37.

As Batman listens hard to try to identify the bizarre noise coming from the fruit, he hears Poison Ivy's harsh laughter from deep in the orchard. He peers into the murk between the trees and catches a glimpse of her slinking down the path in the distance.

Frustrated because he hasn't caught Poison Ivy yet, Batman fights the urge to rush into the orchard after her.

But he knows some kind of trick is waiting for him. How did Poison Ivy booby-trap the fruit trees?

If Batman tries to sneak through the trees unseen by Poison Ivy, turn to page 33.

If Batman tests the path before entering the orchard, turn to page 62.

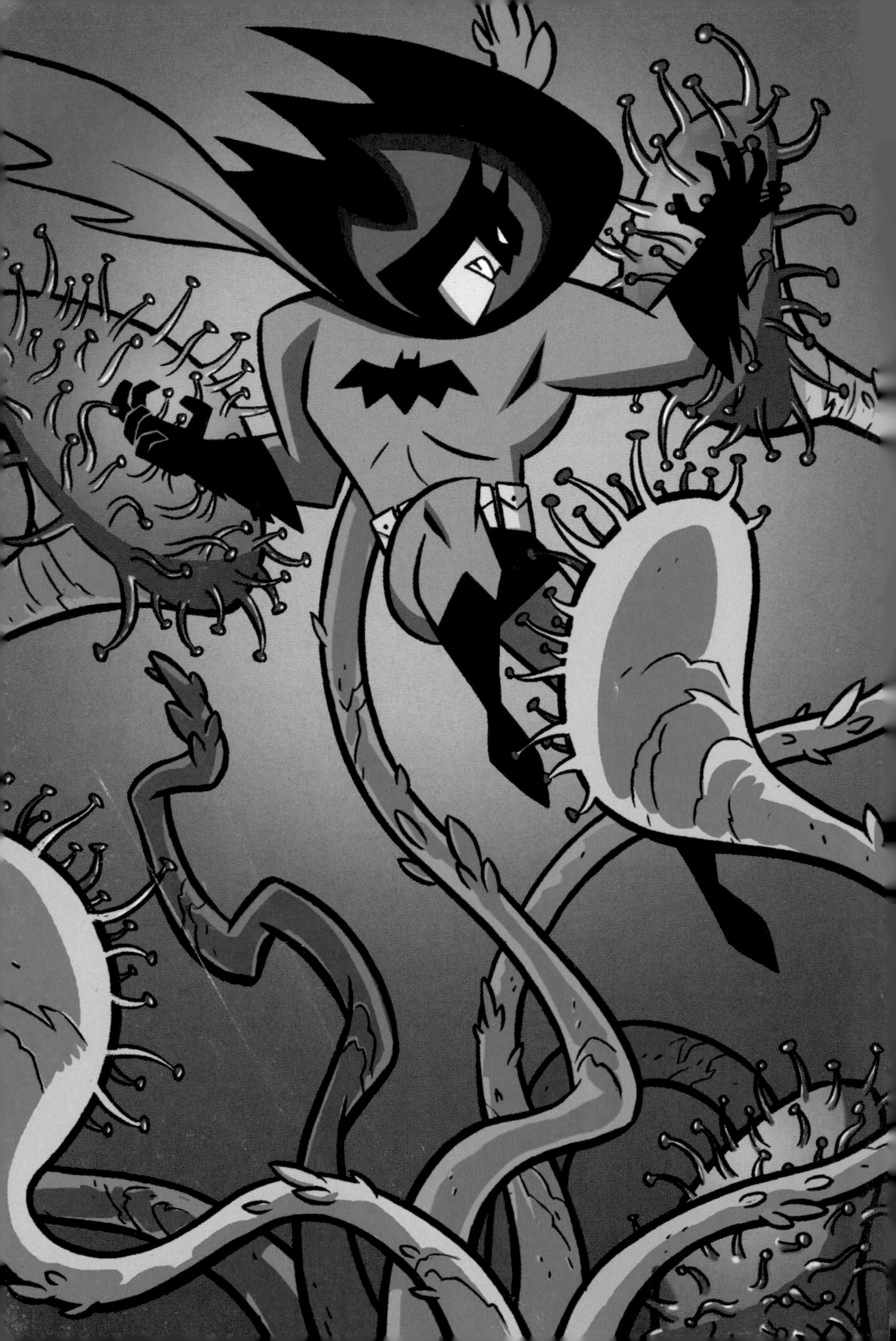

Batman smashes his elbows back, tearing open the sides of the pitcher plant. It's just a curled leaf, after all, no matter how big.

He rips himself completely out of the plant, springing backwards.

Unfortunately, Batman uses more force than is needed to pull free. He stumbles back, smacking his shoulder into the massive sundew plant behind him.

The sundew's tentacles close around his upper arm. Each frond is coated with sticky dew and tangling hairs. The plant starts pulling Batman in closer, tighter.

He can't get away no matter how much he struggles. In his Utility Belt, he has a stun gun, which might affect the sundew plant. Or he could use a Batarang to slice the sticky plant's grip.

If Batman uses his stun gun against the sundew, turn to page 46.
If he cuts the sundew's sticky tentacles, turn to page 89.

As Batman runs into the lilac bushes, he spots Poison Ivy escaping out the other side. The purple vapours surround him, making him feel lightheaded again. He has to follow Ivy, but she's getting too far ahead!

Batman pulls out a strike-anywhere match from a waterproof tube on his Utility Belt. He strikes it on his glove. The match's sulphur-coated tip sparks, and the phosphorus flares into flame. A familiar rotten-egg odour of sulphur dioxide fills Batman's nostrils. He can no longer smell the lilacs!

Free of the dizzying stink, Batman charges through the bushes.

As he crests a small hill, he sees Poison Ivy sneaking through an iron gate into the rose garden.

Turn to page 40.

Sprinting over to the nearest giant carrot, Batman hops up on to the edges of its box. He pulls on the stem with all his might.

The carrot pulls free. Batman struggles to hold it up – it's nearly as tall as he is!

Behind him, the students cheer as Batman tucks the enormous carrot under his arm like a medieval knight in a tournament. He's ready for the first vast tomato when it rolls free.

Batman stabs the gigantic tomato with his carrot lance. The tomato bursts, red juice splashing everywhere.

"My luscious tomato!" Poison Ivy screams. "How dare you!"

Turn to page 94.

The cucumbers grow to the size of sofas. The celery stalks swell into tree trunks. Carrots lump up from the dirt, their orange tops as big as pitcher's mounds. Closest to Batman are the tomatoes, which become the size of boulders. They teeter in their planting box, threatening to roll off and flatten the students.

The cucumber and tomato vines wriggle towards Batman, multiplying madly, attempting to tangle up everybody.

"Stop this, Ivy!" shouts Batman. "These are innocent schoolchildren!"

Poison Ivy laughs. "They need to learn to love their vegetables."

"This is my nightmare!" one boy wails.

"Don't panic," says Batman. He glances around. What can he use to battle the giant vegetables and their vines?

If Batman uses a giant carrot as a joust, turn to page 19.
If he makes a break for the tractor, turn to page 98.

With a wild leap, Batman dashes dozens of aloe plants to the ground as he grabs the edge of the table and flips it sideways, landing in a crouch behind it.

The cacti's needles ricochet off the tabletop. Batman huddles completely safe behind it.

Poison Ivy knows better than to waste her cacti's ammunition. "Hide back there forever!" she hollers, and she strides over to the far corner of the desert environment.

The elevator down to the seed bank vault is open and ready for her. It's unprotected since she already sent the guard running.

"Stick Batman full of holes if he gets up," Poison Ivy instructs her cacti.

The super-villain steps inside the elevator and waves goodbye to Batman as the doors close behind her.

Turn to page 87.

Only a few yards along the path between the pine trees, Poison Ivy steps out from behind a tree. She smiles. "Once these magnificent beings covered vast swaths of the earth. Each may live thousands of years, longer than whole human civilizations. Now they're endangered by deforestation, by human greed."

"I'm as eager to protect pine trees as you are," replies Batman. "You're endangering them with your lawlessness right now."

Poison Ivy's eyes blaze with fury. "You're the one who's endangered, Batman," she says. "But not by the giants."

She raises her hands.

The ferns on either side of Batman stiffen, then grow wildly, tripling in size. The ferns unfurl their fiddleheads towards him, trying to grab him in their feathery grasp.

If Batman climbs a pine tree to escape the grasping ferns, turn to page 43.

If he tries to run from them, turn to page 86.

Batman considers the glue on the tentacles holding him. Their stickiness comes from mucilage, probably intensely acidic so that it can digest its prey with enzymes.

Since the glue has acid in it, Batman realizes that he can neutralize the mucilage with base chemicals ... like calcium ... or ...

With his free hand, Batman reaches into his Utility Belt and grabs a simple antacid tablet. It's not a weapon ... it soothes an upset stomach!

Batman crushes the chalky tablet in his fingers and sprinkles the dust on the sundew.

His arm slides free and then his leg.

Alarmed that Batman has beaten her carnivorous plants, Poison Ivy flees into the desert environment through another tunnel.

Turn to page 51.

Batman stops at the edge of the fruit tree orchard. Up ahead, pear, apple, plum and peach trees grow in rows with a winding path cutting through the middle. The trees are close together in the orchard, and the dense canopy of leaves casts the path in eerie shadow. It's very quiet inside, except for an odd, buzzing hum.

Approaching the nearest pear tree, Batman carefully leans his ear near a low-hanging fruit.

Yes, the noise is coming from the pear. The same weird rumble issues from the apples, plums and peaches, too. The fruit quivers on its stems.

All of Batman's instincts suggest danger. Something isn't right with this orchard.

Turn to page 15.

Beyond the vault door, the seed bank is a high-tech clean room like a laboratory. It's refrigerated to a chill. The walls are lined with metal shelves full of labelled tubes and jars of seeds. A table with microscopes and centrifuges is next to an open, refrigerator-sized box with frosty vapour issuing from it. Poison Ivy has run to the back, where she inspects small cabinet drawers.

Underneath the lab table, a scientist cowers.

Batman hurries to her. "Are you all right?"

"Be careful, Batman," the scientist replies. "That crazy woman interrupted me when I was using the deep freeze for tissue samples. It's really dangerous!"

"Thanks," says Batman. "Now I suggest you run."

The scientist leaps into the elevator and goes up.

Turn to page 74.

Batman kicks at Poison Ivy, but he's pushed back by a blast of crab apple petals. He struggles to stay upright in the flowers whipping around him. It's impossible to see in the swirling pink blizzard. Batman staggers blindly, not sure where Ivy is anymore.

The petals stick to Batman's face, clogging his nose. He spits out bitter flowers, but they're replaced by more. He gags, choking on the petals. The crab apple blossoms smother him.

Batman, suffocating, crumples to the ground and blacks out.

He wakes in the hospital with a nurse peering at him.

"What … time is it?" moans Batman. "Where's Poison Ivy?"

Commissioner Gordon leans into Batman's view. "You've been out for hours," he says grimly. "Ivy robbed the seed bank. She got away."

THE END

To follow another path, turn to page 7.

Batman jumps over to the shelves and starts spilling the most common seeds he can find. He empties jars of sunflower seeds, pumpkin seeds, chickpeas, lima beans, wild rice, barley and tangerine seeds into the gurgling wave of sap.

"Stop that!" screams Poison Ivy. "You're destroying them!"

"You're the one who made this mess," says Batman. "Call off your date palm!"

Coated in seeds, the flow of sap from the date palm slows and stops.

Poison Ivy's red hair sticks out wildly in fury. "You shouldn't have threatened their futures," she says. "Now it's time to get serious."

Turn to page 91.

The hanging plants and vines on the banyan tree wriggle and grow behind Poison Ivy. "Meet my epiphytes," she says. "They're quite wonderful, living on other plants, but getting their nutrients and water from the air. Some air plants have roots that choke other trees, like my favourite, the strangler fig."

"I know epiphytes," growls Batman. He backs up as the strangler fig species extends grasping, hairy roots towards him.

"I'd love to watch what happens when a strangler fig overtakes a Batman," says Poison Ivy.

Batman glances around to see what he can use to fight. There's a garden hose nearby, but he might be better off simply using his acrobatic skills to avoid the reaching roots.

If Batman flips away acrobatically, turn to page 49.
If he uses the hose on the epiphytes, turn to page 85.

With Poison Ivy viciously attacking, Batman can't be bothered by the stink of the lilacs. He blocks her swinging fists with his gauntlets, pushing her back with his greater strength.

Almost faster than Batman can track, Poison Ivy cartwheels towards him, kicking at his midsection.

Batman jumps back just in time, feeling lightheaded. Maybe the lilac odour is getting to him.

Gritting his teeth, Batman twirls his cape, swirling purple mist. The cape also might misdirect Ivy, perhaps confusing her so he can land a punch.

No such luck. Poison Ivy spots his trick, and she flips away from his fist.

Batman charges at her but stops ... he's feeling dizzy again from the cloying smell of the flowers.

If Batman toughs out the woozy feeling, turn to page 48.
If Batman stops fighting to put on his oxygen mask, turn to page 88.

It's dim, cool, and quiet inside the crab apple grove. The sunlight filters in pinkish, and the air smells too sweet.

When nothing jumps out at him, Batman advances along the path in Ivy's direction.

In the centre of the grove, Batman stops when a funnel of petals starts whirling in front of him.

The pink tornado of petals spins faster. Poison Ivy steps out of the floral flurry. "I adore how the prettiest things can be the most deadly," she hisses.

"Whatever you're planning," Batman warns, "don't do it."

Poison Ivy raises her arms.

If Batman hangs back to see what Poison Ivy does, turn to page 82.

If Batman rushes at her, turn to page 100.

Although he can't trust Poison Ivy, Batman believes he can handle the ruby dragon. He chomps it.

It's sweet like chocolate and cherries.

Then the spice detonates like a supernova. His tongue and lips blaze, and the insides of his cheeks scorch with heat. The chilli inferno whooshes into his sinuses, frying his nasal passages, sizzling his ears. The bite of pepper lodges in his chest, radiating pulses of fire.

Gasping for air, blinded by agony, Batman slumps off the shelves.

He blacks out before he hits the floor.

Batman wakes in a hospital with a nurse smiling down at him. "You're lucky to be alive," she says.

"No thanks to Poison Ivy," says Batman.

Someday, he swears, he will get revenge.

THE END

To follow another path, turn to page 7.

Batman pulls a spool of thread from his Utility Belt and ties one end to a hedge. He lets the thread unravel behind him as he walks deeper into the maze.

"Might as well take all right turns," says Batman.

He spots Poison Ivy disappearing around a corner, so he charges after her. Her laughter carries through the hedges, but she's not around the next turn, or the next.

At a three-way intersection, Batman pauses, using his tracking skills. He spots a footprint in the middle path's wood chips. He heads in that direction, his thread trailing behind.

Then he finds his own thread at the next turn. It leads straight through a hedge wall.

"Thread is useless when Ivy's moving walls," grumbles Batman. "I'm lost."

Turn to page 36.

A lifetime of sneaking up on criminals in his patrols of Gotham City prepared Batman to move quickly and quietly, staying hidden in the shadows. His stealth training sometimes comes in very handy.

The spooky orchard is no different. He moves silently but surely, sliding from pear tree to apple tree to peach tree without a whisper of sound. His boots barely dent the underbrush as he glides closer to Poison Ivy.

From his hiding spot behind a leafy peach tree, he spots her across the path sniffing a plum blossom.

With a powerful leap, Batman may be able to reach Poison Ivy from where he's concealed in the shadows. Or should he try to make it closer first and move behind a nearby pear tree?

If Batman leaps at Poison Ivy, turn to page 56.
If he keeps sneaking closer, turn to page 81.

Peony flowers bloom on hedges of waist-high shrubs, winding in rows along a hill's slope. Batman pads along a path, planning to sneak up on Poison Ivy around the next corner.

The many huge peony blossoms are impressive, each as wide as a cereal bowl, with giant petals fluttering like crepe paper. Their scent is sharp and delicate.

Bees buzz by, alighting in the white, pink, yellow and red blooms.

Batman stops short by a shrub with crimson flowers. Poison Ivy stands at the end of the row, her hands on her hips.

"You're never going to stop following me, are you?" she demands.

"No," replies Batman. "Not until you're back in Arkham."

"Then I need help," says Poison Ivy.

Turn to page 80.

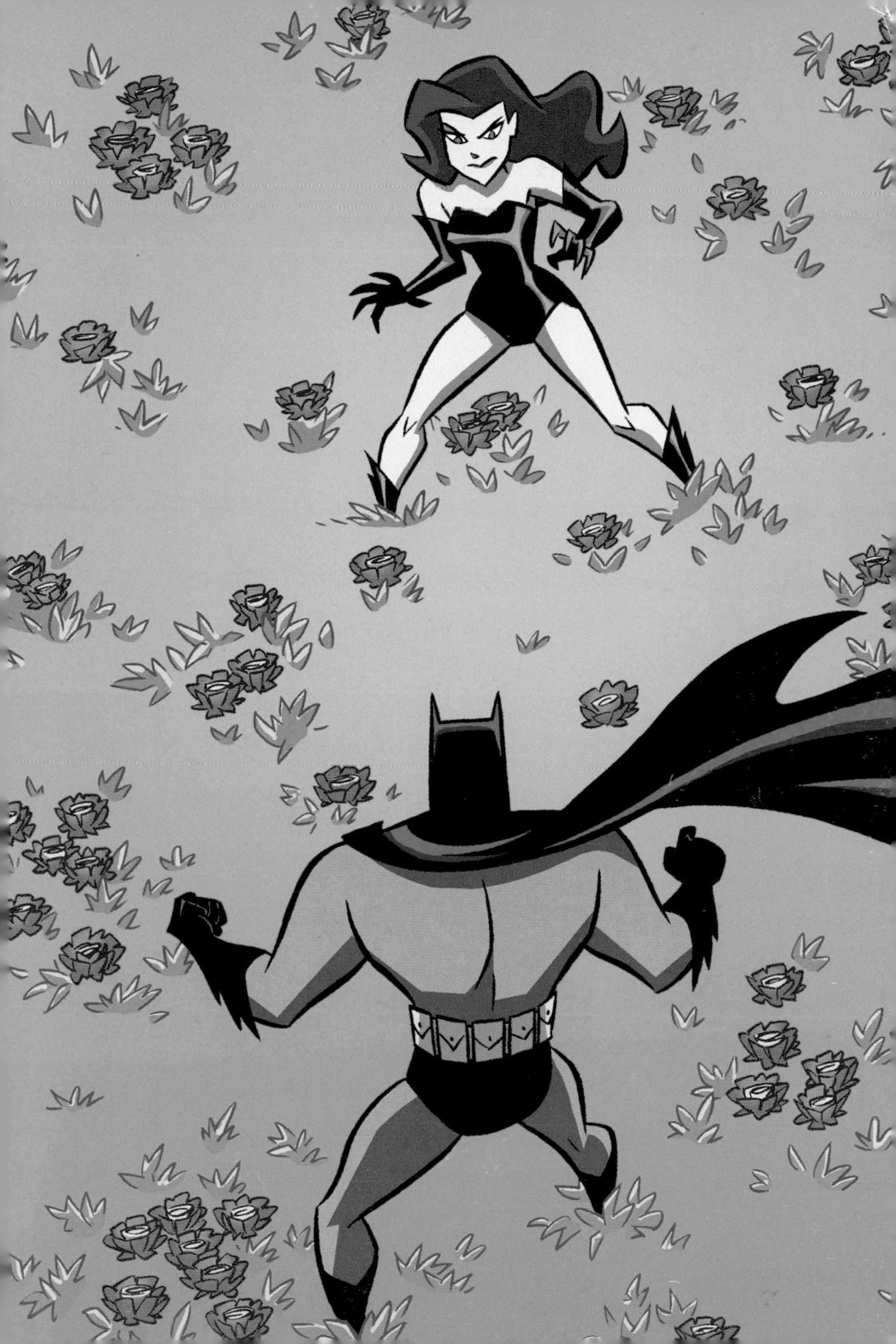

Certain that he can find the exit if he makes surprising turns, Batman keeps trying to escape the maze. He takes different pathways and circles back for hours until he's completely and utterly lost in the labyrinth.

The shadows of the hedges grow longer as the day gets later. Poison Ivy must have left the maze by now. "Obviously, she left the vegetation in the maze on autopilot," says Batman. "It's moving around automatically without her."

As soon as he says that, he turns a corner and finds the exit.

Batman rushes out of the hedge maze and finds two policeman on the lawn.

"Poison Ivy robbed the seed bank and got away!" says one cop. "Where were you?"

"I was lost," replies Batman.

THE END

To follow another path, turn to page 7.

A curvy, green woman with red hair emerges from a thicket of puffy purple hydrangeas. Poison Ivy glares at Batman.

"Give yourself up, Ivy!" he hollers. "Before anyone gets hurt. You're going back to Arkham anyway."

"Never will I return to that sunless dungeon, Batman," replies Poison Ivy. "I must free the future of the world's flora."

"The seed bank is crucial to humanity's survival after a disaster," says Batman. "I can't allow you to control it."

Poison Ivy sniffs a droopy orange honeysuckle flower on a squat bush. "It is not necessarily your decision, Batman," she says. "I believe I am the authority on the treatment of plants. Do not hinder me, or it will be your doom."

"Stay where you are," orders Batman.

Turn to page 84.

Hunkered in the middle of the gazebo, the old man and woman cling to one another. Brambles tangle around the shelter like flowering tentacles.

In moments, the structure is encircled by thorny vines. Red and yellow roses pulsate along the briar. It's too dangerous to be beautiful.

"In your last moments of life," calls Poison Ivy from outside, "don't forget to smell the roses!" Her wicked laugh fades into the distance as she strides away.

"We'll die in here," the old woman wails.

"Nobody's going to die," says Batman.

He takes inventory of his Utility Belt. Maybe he can do something with his grapnel gun? Or perhaps he can use a jagged plank of the wooden trellis as a machete.

If Batman tries to hack through the brambles with the broken board, turn to page 44.

If he uses his grapnel gun, turn to page 52.

Batman pulls Batarangs out of a Utility Belt pouch and flings them at the banana missiles. He has had so much practice throwing Batarangs that he hurls them almost automatically.

He hits the first barrage of bananas, slicing them up and knocking them off course.

But the banana missiles keep coming. One gets through, smacking Batman on his shoulder with a splat.

Then Batman runs out of Batarangs.

A dozen bananas bonk him on the head, knocking him unconscious.

Batman is woken up hours later by a botanical garden guard. "What ... what happened?" Batman asks.

"Poison Ivy stole every seed in the seed bank," the guard replies.

Batman shakes his sore head. It's so embarrassing to have been beaten by bananas.

THE END

To follow another path, turn to page 7.

Batman dashes down the hill along the path towards the rose garden.

A high ironwork fence surrounds the whole garden in a giant hexagon, with an open arched gate on each of the six sides. Climbing vines covered in a riot of roses intertwine with the iron lattice fencing all around.

Now that Poison Ivy has entered, the roses throb pink, red, orange, yellow and white, a wild kaleidoscope of floral colour.

Batman pauses at the gate, peering at the paths lined with white pebbles through trellises of buds and blossoms, all leading to a central domed gazebo.

Roses have tangling vines and intoxicating scents.

Roses have severely sharp thorns.

Roses are dangerous.

Turn to page 90.

Batman can't get involved in boxing the saguaro. The possibility of damage to himself and the innocent plant is too high. So he turns and runs, bolting around a set of display tables covered in pots of jagged aloe plants.

"Get ready!" Poison Ivy calls to her army of cacti around the room. "Volley!"

At her command, the cacti fire spines at Batman.

As Batman glances around, trying to figure out how to escape the hundreds of spiny missiles heading in his direction, another saguaro throws a punch at his face.

If Batman uses the saguaro as a shield, turn to page 71.
If he twirls himself up in his cape, turn to page 99.

Batman scrambles up the hill after Poison Ivy.

The Greenhouse Conservatory is a huge complex of connected glass rooms, each with a different climate-controlled environment inside. It houses rare and unique plants from around the world, including a whole wing for carnivorous plants and a desert environment for cacti.

Batman seriously hopes he can stop Poison Ivy before she reaches the carnivorous plant room!

The Wayne Seed Bank is located in a vast bunker underneath the conservatory. It can only be reached from a guarded elevator in the desert environment.

Poison Ivy yanks open the Greenhouse's front door and slips inside.

Batman follows her less than three minutes later.

Turn to page 70.

Batman can't waste time fighting crazy ferns. He yanks a long wire out of his Utility Belt and swings it around a pine tree trunk. With ferns snapping at his boots, Batman hoists himself up.

He finds footing on the bark, and then flips the rope higher to pull up the next step.

Batman climbs steadily, far off the forest floor.

Mists swirl around him, and he feels the wind rushing by. "Don't look down," he reminds himself.

He reaches the first level of branches, eighty feet off the ground. Now he can swing through the pine tree canopy. In a short time, he reaches the edge of the grove.

From his great height, he can see Poison Ivy running into the hedge maze nearby.

Turn to page 75.

With a jagged piece of wooden plank, Batman hacks at the thorny vines. Rose petals fly everywhere.

A vine studded with orange rosebuds swoops over and wraps around the board. Batman wrestles with the vine, but it yanks the plank from his grip.

"Get down!" Batman orders the old couple.

They huddle on the gazebo floor. Batman covers them with his body, his cape stiffening around them all to form a tight protective dome.

He feels the vines twisting around them, thorns scraping against his tough cape.

They're unhurt ... but trapped.

It takes hours for rescue workers to cut them out of the bramble of roses, and by that time, Poison Ivy is long gone with the precious seeds from the seed bank.

THE END

To follow another path, turn to page 7.

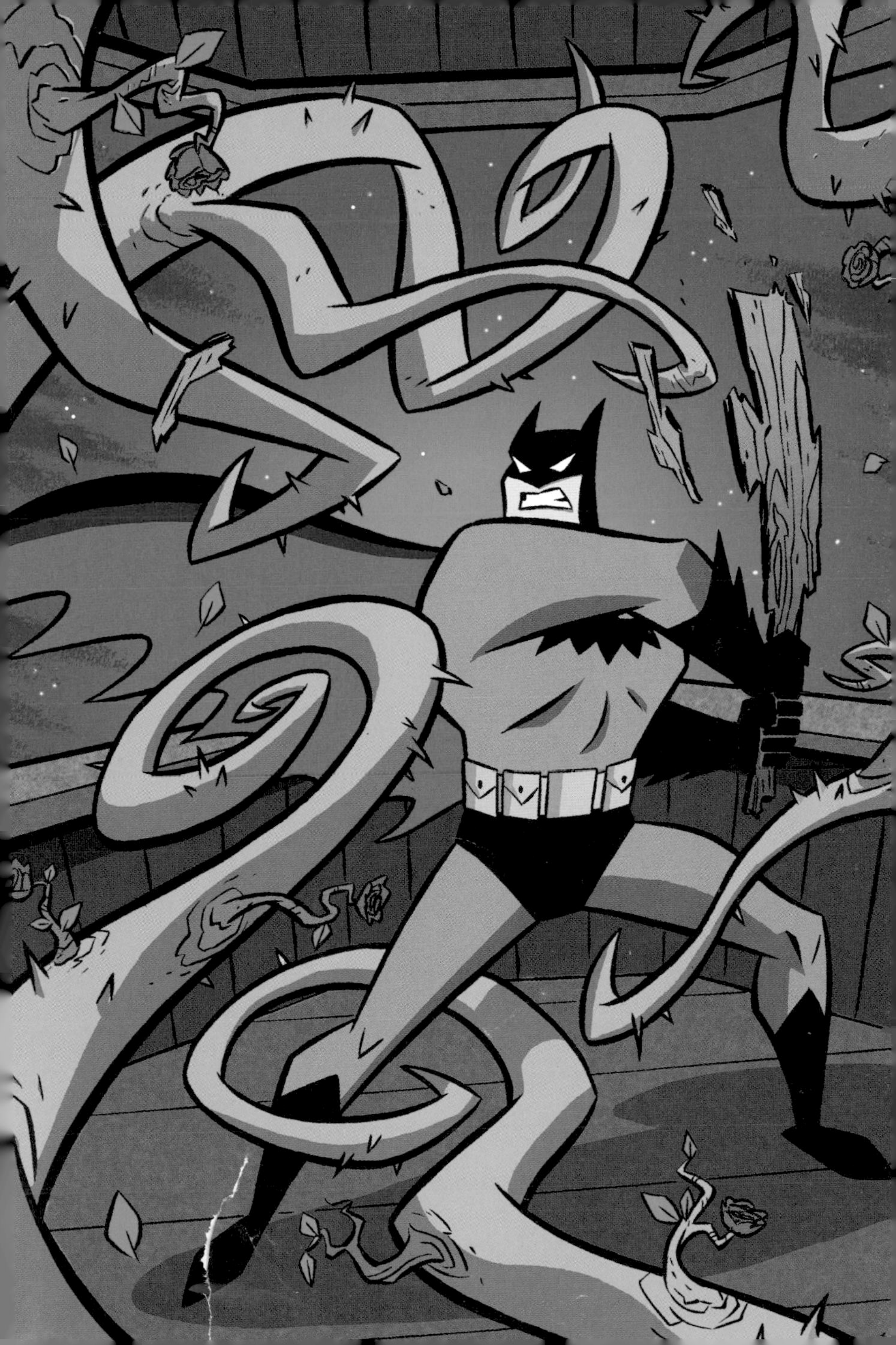

With his free hand, Batman pulls his stun gun from his Utility Belt. It's not strong enough to kill anyone or anything, but it does send out a shock that can paralyse weak creatures.

He points the stun gun at the writhing sundew and pulls the trigger.

Blue electricity zips all over the sundew's tentacles, flashing and reflecting in its sticky beads of liquid.

The stun gun has no effect on the plant whatsoever.

Instead, the sundew grabs Batman's leg with its tentacles and binds them tight.

"All right, then," says Batman. "On to Plan B."

If Batman tries to neutralize the sundew's glue chemically, turn to page 23.

If he slices the sundew's tentacles with a Batarang, turn to page 89.

With a sharp slap, Batman smacks his chin. Instantly, his face swarms with bees. Insects sting his nose, lips, cheeks, chin and neck.

Batman gasps, and bees buzz inside his mouth, stinging his tongue.

The hero swats the bugs from his face, but more replace those he slaps away. The bees inject their venom into Batman's skin.

He passes out from the poison and shock.

Batman wakes up in the Batcave, with his butler Alfred peering down at him.

"Oh, good, Master Bruce," says Alfred, "you're alive."

Batman tries to reply, but his lips are too swollen for him to speak.

It will take weeks for him to fully recover.

THE END

To follow another path, turn to page 7.

The reek of flowers is no reason to give up. Batman's stronger than the smell of lilacs!

He feints left to catch Poison Ivy off guard, but she flees into the blossoming bushes.

The lavender blooms tremble, and a fog of purple odour surrounds Batman. He fans it away, but his eyes roll up in his head. He crumples to the damp ground, blacking out.

He wakes with two policemen dragging him from the lilac bushes. "How long was I unconscious?" asks Batman.

"Hours," says the skinnier cop. "We tried to stop Poison Ivy at the conservatory, but she escaped underground with all the seeds."

Batman winces. He has a terrible headache … and he'll never sneer at the power of flowers again!

THE END

To follow another path, turn to page 7.

With graceful acrobatic moves, Batman
flips on his hands, then back again on his feet,
twisting in the air, avoiding the attacks.

He rolls low, cartwheels, and does a
roundhouse flip, so no plant can take aim at him
or even get close.

But, being so busy flipping around, he can't
capture Poison Ivy, either.

She zooms out of the tropical room ... down
a glass tunnel towards the carnivorous plant
environment.

Batman grits his teeth, then ducks and rolls,
reaching the exit so he can chase her.

Turn to page 105.

Batman jumps over vine tendrils and wraps his arms around a celery stalk as high as he can reach.

The celery bends, then catapults him across the garden. He soars over the vegetables, landing on top of the tractor.

"You used my own celery against me!" seethes Poison Ivy.

With a stomp on the pedals, the tractor roars to life.

"Time to make a salad," says Batman. He steers the tractor into the garden, slicing vines, chopping up cucumbers and shredding lettuce. Chunks of vegetables fly everywhere.

Poison Ivy shrieks when she sees Batman heading for her on the tractor.

The students behind Batman cheer as he chases her out of the vegetable garden towards the orchard.

Turn to page 24.

The final greenhouse room houses a desert environment. It's hot and dry, and filled with plants that don't need much moisture, including puffy succulents, fan palms and spiny cacti.

It's the last category that worries Batman. The cacti can be deadly weapons.

Through the glass wall, he sees the seed bank elevator's guard running away with spines jabbed in his behind.

Batman's uniform has a tight alloy weave that can withstand some cactus needles. He must pay most attention to protecting the part of his face that's exposed below his mask.

"Ivy!" Batman calls. "Before you go too far, let's discuss this reasonably. We can come to an understanding, perhaps a seed sharing agreement."

"You sound frightened, Batman," replies Poison Ivy.

"Not me," says Batman. "Never."

Turn to page 102.

Batman climbs to the gazebo's ceiling and kicks a hole in the roof. He sees a sturdy tree limb looming high above.

After aiming with his grapnel gun, Batman shoots a hook. Its wire winds around the tree limb, snagging tight. Batman connects his end to the roof.

"Hold on," Batman tells the senior couple. They grab support beams.

Batman activates the grapnel gun's winch. With a shuddering lurch, the wire hoists the gazebo off its foundation. The old woman screams. Rose vines rip away.

The gazebo tears free, rising to the tree limb, where it dangles like a birdcage.

Batman spots Poison Ivy's red hair. She's running towards the vegetable garden nearby.

"Excuse me," Batman says to the seniors. "Someone will rescue you soon."

He swings down and chases after Poison Ivy.

Turn to page 104.

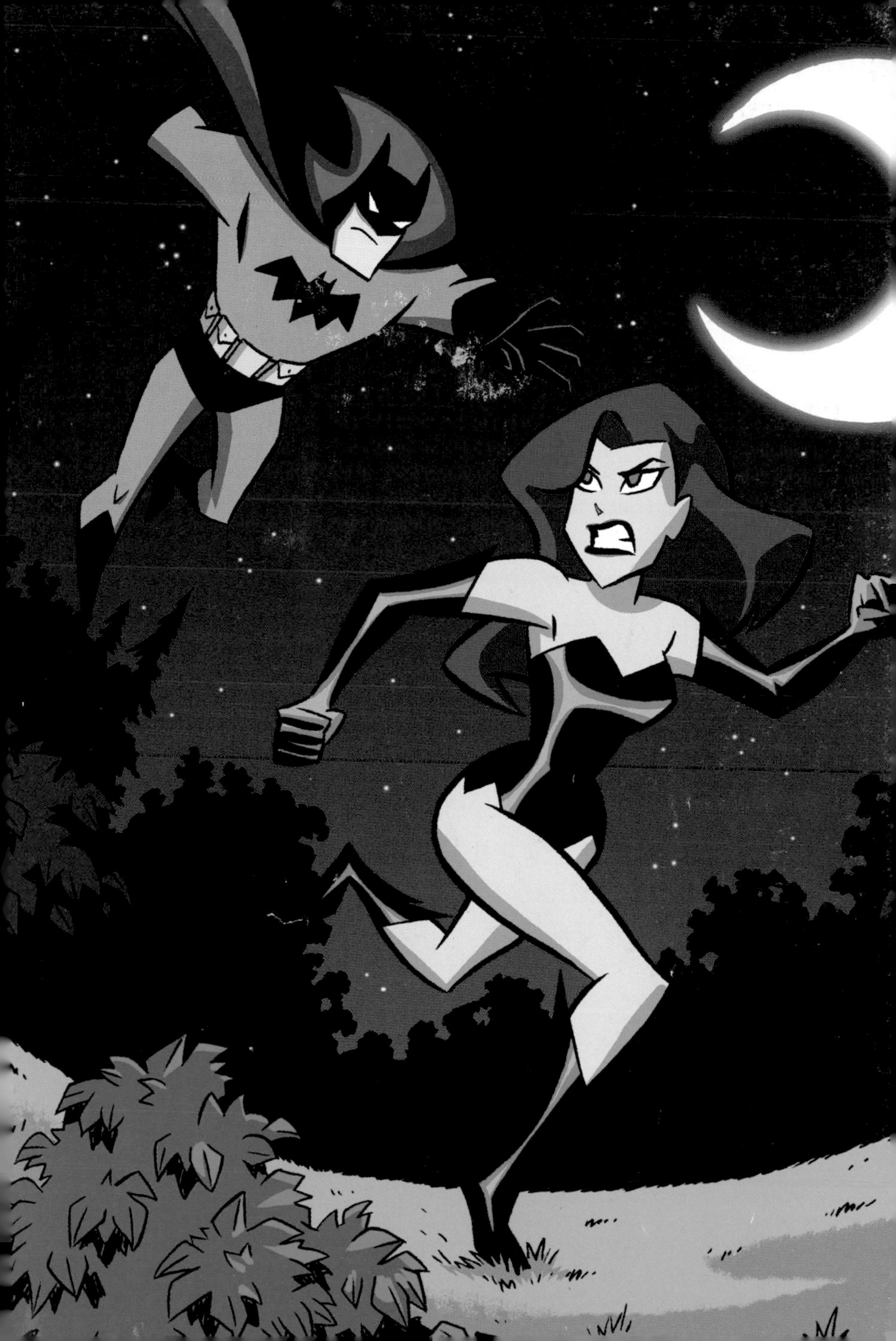

Batman charges along the path towards a hill dotted with dozens of flowering crab apple trees. The low, spiky branches are heavy with masses of delicate pink petals.

At the edge of the crab apple grove, Batman skids to a halt. It isn't smart to rush under the blossoming canopy in the tight little orchard. He squats and tilts his head to peer around the trees' spindly trunks.

A few yards in, Poison Ivy shifts out from behind a cluster of crab apple trees. She spots Batman and scowls. Then she darts deeper into the grove, disappearing behind a wall of dense petals.

Batman knows it's dangerous to chase her, but he can't let her escape.

Turn to page 30.

Batman walks into the maze until he reaches the first choice of paths, left or right.

"How will I know the paths I've taken?" he wonders aloud. "It's easy to get lost."

Batman remembers the ancient Greek myth of Theseus and the Minotaur. Theseus had the task of killing the half-man, half-bull Minotaur in a dark maze. A woman named Ariadne suggested that Theseus unravel a ball of string as he went into the labyrinth, which helped him find his way out after he slew the monster.

"I have thread in my Utility Belt," says Batman.

Batman also has a communicator, which connects to a GPS satellite. He could use the high-tech device instead.

If Batman strings a thread along the path, turn to page 32.
If he uses his GPS technology, turn to page 77.

Batman zeroes in on Poison Ivy's red hair, which he can see through the fruit trees, and he barrels towards her at full speed.

When he gets close enough, he leaps as hard as he can, his arms outstretched for a clothes-line tackle.

A deafening explosion erupts all around. The fruit in the trees in front of him detonates like dynamite, spraying pulp into his face. The blast is strong enough to flatten Batman to the ground, and he loses all the air in his lungs when he thumps down hard. Then he's conked in the head by dozens of peach and plum pits, knocking him unconscious.

Batman wakes up hours later in a sticky mess of fruit gunk.

Poison Ivy is long gone.

THE END

To follow another path, turn to page 7.

"I don't believe you," Poison Ivy says, laughing. "You think of yourself as an independent creature, above the law, but really you fight for terrible injustice."

"That's not true," replies Batman.

"Yes, it is!" insists Poison Ivy. She slinks closer to him, the ruby dragon chilli pepper tapping against Batman's lips. "You seek to keep plants locked in eternal slavery to humanity! This is a crime against nature!"

"I see your point," says Batman, although he realizes how crazy and dangerous Poison Ivy really is. "Get this pepper out of my face and we'll fight for the rights of plants."

"Like all humans, you lie," she seethes. "Which is more important, liberating plants from slavery, or feeding the world's people by farming my friends?"

If Batman says farming is more important, turn to page 66.

If he says all plants should be free from human control, turn to page 101.

Batman dashes to the shelves, scrambling to the top of the fifth shelf.

Poison Ivy tosses seeds up around him. "These ruby dragon peppers may not be good climbers, but that doesn't matter if they're already up there."

The seeds sprout, maturing fast and growing fiery red fruit. The plants creep along the shelf towards Batman, reaching his legs.

"They hold the record for hottest chilli," adds Poison Ivy. "I'll enjoy watching you burn up."

Backed into a corner, Batman kicks at the explosive pepper plants, but they twine up his body. They wrap stems around his neck, strangling him.

A shiny ruby dragon chilli dangles by Batman's mouth.

"Eat it," says Poison Ivy. "If you survive, I'll let you live."

If Batman bites the pepper, turn to page 31.
If he tries to reason with Poison Ivy, turn to page 95.

"These are only plants!" shouts Batman. He punches the fern.

His fist sinks into the ferns, and he yanks the plant apart.

The fern chomps Batman's shoulder from behind. Its leaves don't break through Batman's cape or costume, but the bite stings.

"That hurt," growls Batman. He kicks the fern, smashing its stems.

Fiddleheads wrap around Batman's ankle. The ferns bind his leg, dragging him into the bushes, where the bigger stems tie his body. In seconds, he can't struggle anymore.

Poison Ivy peers down at Batman. "So ferns are stronger than bats," she says, and leaves him lying there.

Batman listens to the creak of the pine trees for hours before he's rescued.

THE END

To follow another path, turn to page 7.

The crab apple hurricane is intense. If Batman doesn't shelter himself, he'll suffocate in the petal maelstrom. He crouches and whirls his cape around him in a protective dome.

Under the cape, Batman can still hear the whipping wind and feel the flowers slamming into him. But he has space to breathe.

After a few minutes, he senses that the stinging petals have stopped swirling. Raising his cape, Batman finds himself under a heap of blossoms. He digs to the surface and gulps in air.

The crab apple trees around him are bare. The ground looks like the aftermath of a pink blizzard.

Batman scans the area and catches a glimpse of Poison Ivy striding through an iron gate, into the rose garden.

Turn to page 40.

The fruit orchard was dark and creepy, but nothing compared to the eerie majesty of the pine tree grove.

Poison Ivy quickly vanishes behind the massive, ancient trees, disappearing into the white mists that swirl around the vast trunks. There's a hush throughout the grove, as though the pine trees are creaking softly in their sleep.

Batman pursues her along the path lined with the feathery fronds of ferns and their furled young leaves called fiddleheads.

He glances up at the dizzying height of the trees, their tops lost in clouds.

He's not sure he wants to find out how Poison Ivy may use these colossal plants against him.

Turn to page 22.

Suspicious of the weirdly buzzing orchard, Batman picks up a pebble and tosses it down the path through the fruit trees.

The pebble bounces once with a clink. Then all the fruit around it explodes in a juicy, violent blast of pears, plums, apples and peaches.

Batman ducks down, protecting his face. Seeds and bits of pit whiz by, tearing up the dirt. There's pulp and sweet shrapnel everywhere.

"Fruit bombs," Batman growls. "I should've known."

He doesn't want to think what would have happened if he'd triggered the explosion with his body. At the very least, it would've been sticky.

Once again, he hears Poison Ivy's irritating laughter from somewhere deep in the orchard.

If Batman decides that it's safe to rush Poison Ivy now, turn to page 56.

If he uses his stealth skills to follow her, turn to page 81.

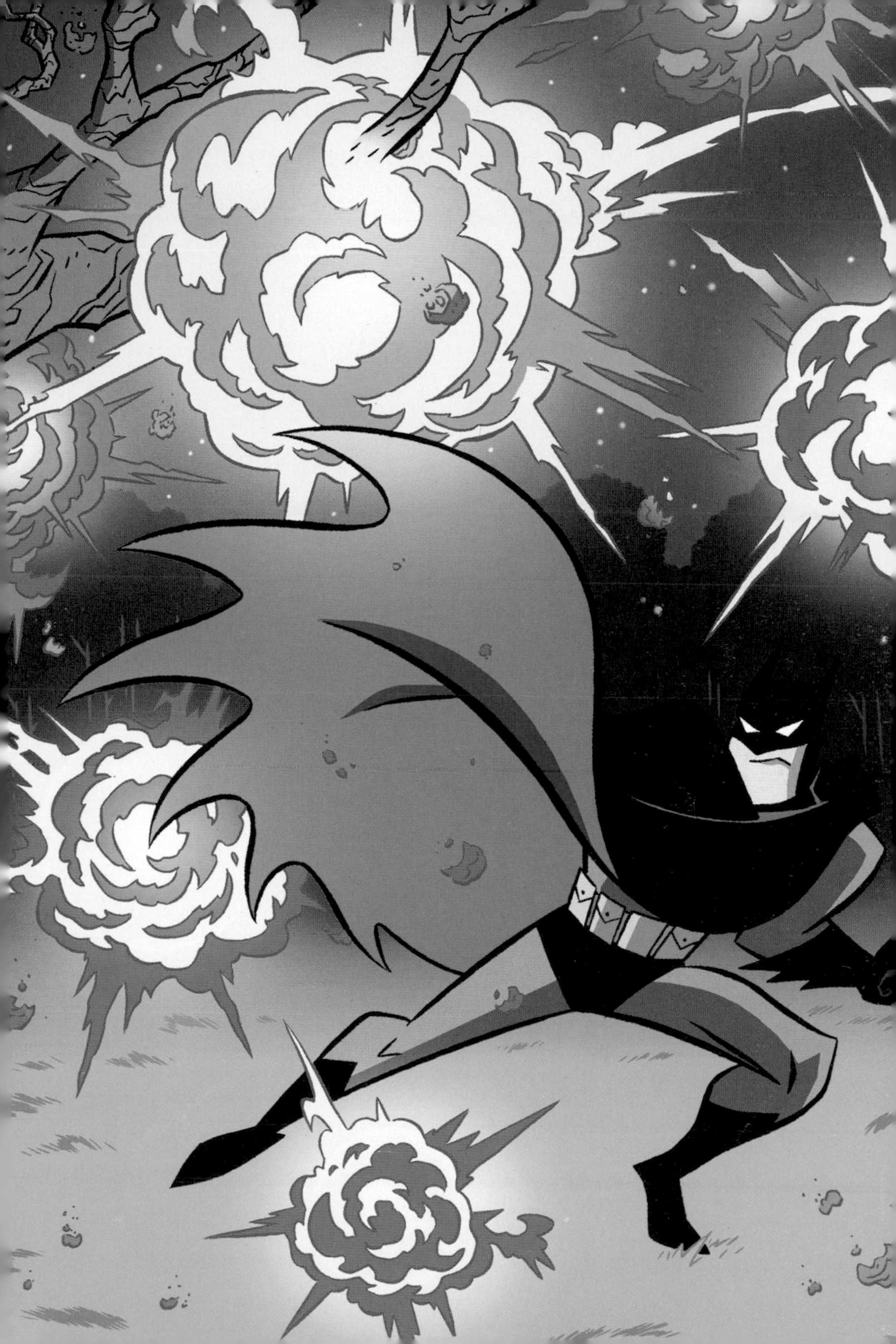

Having had enough of glue for the moment, Batman turns towards the vase-shaped pitcher plant towering to his left. It reeks of sweet nectar. Insects are attracted to the scent, and they get tricked into the pitcher. They drown in the liquid inside, and the plant digests them.

"But nectar does nothing for me," says Batman. He starts to kick the pitcher plant, but its leaves push him from behind. He topples inside the pitcher plant's tube.

Batman wedges his elbows against the walls, holding himself up above the plant's digestive liquid. His legs waggle upside-down in the air.

Poison Ivy laughs. "You're as snug as a bug in there," she says. "Enjoy being eaten."

"I am not a bug," he growls. "I am Batman."

Turn to page 17.

Batman yanks the criss-crossed wooden trellis off the gazebo's side.

"What do you plan to do with that, young Batman?" asks the old man.

"Roses climb trellises," answers Batman. "You two stay close behind me."

He holds the six-foot interwoven support in front of him. With the senior couple following, Batman steps from the gazebo in the direction he heard Poison Ivy's laugh.

A vine studded with orange rosebuds whips out and snares the bottom of the trellis.

Batman points the support away, and the vine climbs it, diverted to the left.

"It's working!" the old woman cheers.

Six more thorny vines snake towards them.

"I can't sidetrack them, too," says Batman.

If Batman hustles the seniors back into the gazebo, turn to page 38.

If he tries to hack through the brambles with a jagged board, turn to page 44.

"So will you move the ruby dragon pepper away from me?" askes Batman.

"Yes," replies Poison Ivy. "But don't think you're safe. Fool, I know better than to trust your words." She smiles wickedly. "Now that I have you at my mercy, you will help me whether you want to or not."

"Poison Ivy," says Batman, "whatever you're planning, we can discuss –"

She leans forward and blows him a kiss.

A faint green cloud flutters into his face, and he can't help inhaling it.

Her kiss is full of her mind-controlling spores. The germs travel into Batman's brain, taking over his thoughts, making his eyes glow toxic green.

Unable to fight Poison Ivy's influence, Batman stands by and watches her rob the seed bank.

THE END

To follow another path, turn to page 7.

With the razor-sharp claws on his gauntlets, Batman hacks at the hedge in the direction of where he saw Poison Ivy on the map.

The hedge fights back, growing wildly to surround Batman, smacking him with twigs, and loosening leaves into his face.

But it's only a hedge, and Batman slices it into submission. He chops through one hedge, and then the next shrubby wall, slashing a diagonal across the maze, ignoring the paths. It doesn't matter if Poison Ivy moves the bushes around if he's cutting straight through them!

It doesn't take long for Batman to hack his way out of the maze.

He sees Poison Ivy fleeing across a wide lawn, towards the massive glass-domed Greenhouse Conservatory atop a wide hill.

Turn to page 42.

Not wanting to startle the bees with any sudden movements, Batman inches towards Poison Ivy.

She watches him approach, her eyes fixed on his. When he's a few steps away, she claps her hands sharply.

Batman winces as a single bee stings his chin. He hunches his shoulders.

That really hurt!

If Batman slaps the stinging bee, turn to page 47.
If he ignores the pain, turn to page 97.

Perhaps if Batman runs fast enough, he can follow the paths he saw on the map before Poison Ivy has time to shift the hedges. The exit is only six turns away.

He rounds a right turn, accelerates down a straightaway, then careens to the left at a T-shaped intersection. According to his memory of the map, he needs to take the next left, then a right, then keep straight...

Batman skids to a halt.

It's a dead end.

Batman races back the way he came. He makes a left at the previous turn, which he remembers also leads to the exit. But two turns later, he hits another dead end.

Nothing he remembers from the map matters. Batman is lost in the labyrinth.

Turn to page 36.

The first environment is the hot tropical jungle room. The air is so humid that the broad-leafed plants drip water down pitted volcanic rocks into a stream in the floor. It smells dank and loamy.

Poison Ivy waits for Batman by a twisted banyan tree covered by vines and dangling, mossy plants. Behind the banyan are tall banana trees. Brilliant orchid flowers are everywhere.

"You believe it was a good idea to follow me here?" asks Poison Ivy. "You are in terrible peril."

Batman feels sweaty in his Batsuit. "I don't have a choice," he replies. "I can't allow you to rob the seed bank."

"I can't allow you to stop me," says Poison Ivy.

She raises her palms, her eyes blazing green.

Turn to page 28.

Batman ducks under the saguaro's spiny punch. He feints left, then plugs his gloved right fist smack into a white flower growing in the cactus's face. The needles poke his fist, but they don't break through the reinforced material over his knuckles.

As the saguaro wobbles, Poison Ivy readies her next attack. Hundreds of cacti plants around the greenhouse point their needles at Batman. "Volley!" she shouts.

Thousands of needles fly through the air at Batman. He jumps behind the saguaro, holding up his arms, hiding in back of the tall cactus as a shield. The other cacti's spikes stick like arrows all over the saguaro. It starts to fall, defeated.

"Volley!" Poison Ivy shouts again.

The cacti let loose another wave of deadly needles.

If Batman overturns a planting table to block the attack, turn to page 21.

If he wraps himself up in his cape, turn to page 99.

Under Poison Ivy's influence, a Venus flytrap swells to enormous size. Its spiky leaf traps loom as large as Batman's head. He backs away as Poison Ivy laughs.

"I am not food," says Batman. He needs to trigger the traps before they latch on to him, but with what?

Rooting around in his Utility Belt, Batman grabs a canister of glue globules. Each pellet is filled with strong glue. "Perfect," he says.

When a trap threatens Batman, he tosses a glue globule into its maw. Soon all the meat-eating plant's traps are glued shut.

Poison Ivy shrieks in frustration.

To the left of Batman, a pitcher plant springs up, growing gigantic and gurgling. On his right, a sundew plant sprouts tall, waving its sticky tentacles.

If Batman attacks the sundew plants, turn to page 46.
If he attacks the pitcher plants, turn to page 64.

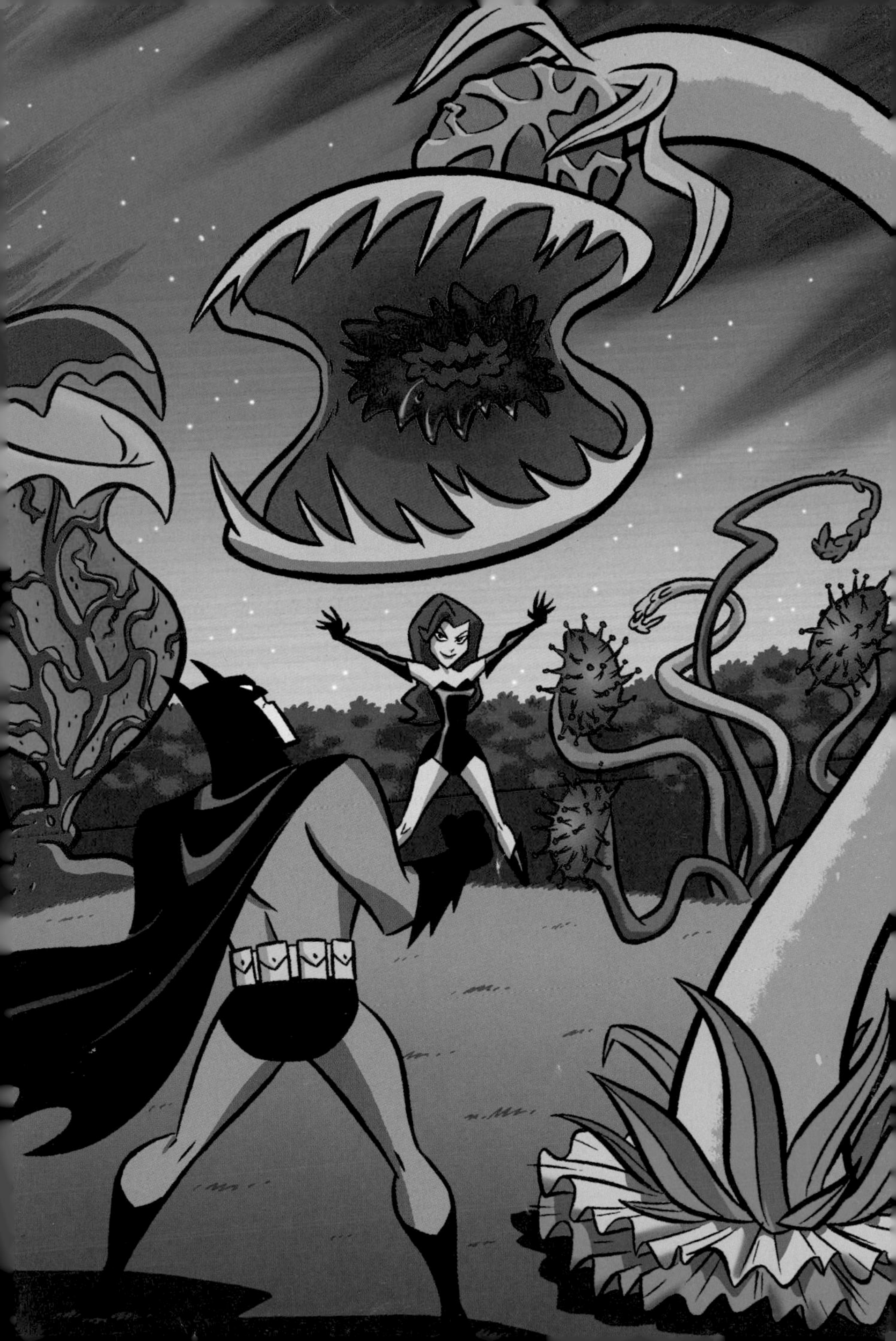

The movement of the elevator gets Poison Ivy's attention. She rushes towards the front of the vault, glaring at Batman.

"You're as persistent as an invasive weed," she seethes. "I've got a history lesson for you."

She throws a seed on the floor in front of Batman. It springs into instant growth, long fronds expanding like an opening fist.

"A date palm," says Batman, recognizing it. "From the oldest seeds in the world."

"Stored more than two thousand years ago," agrees Poison Ivy. "As alive as ever."

With astounding speed, the short palm tree grows bundles of sweet-smelling fruit hanging like grapes. The dates quickly pop, spurting sticky sap on to the floor.

They spew so much goo that it oozes towards Batman's boots.

If Batman spills seeds to coat the sap, turn to page 27.
If he climbs the shelves to escape, turn to page 58.

Poison Ivy bolts through the arched entranceway to the hedge maze. The walls, made of yew trees, are nine feet high and four feet wide and trimmed into dense shrubs.

Batman follows her into the maze, which is sunny and quiet, with soft wood chips covering the path. He hears a rustling noise.

Behind him, the entranceway's arch fills in with branches and leaves, growing closed. In seconds, there is no trace of it having existed at all.

"Poison Ivy can move the walls around," Batman says with a groan. "This is going to be a-maze-ing!"

Turn to page 55.

Batman snaps the stem of the ruby dragon pepper and throws his body against Poison Ivy.

She stumbles backwards, falling into the open chamber of the flash-freeze apparatus.

Batman slams the door shut.

"Release me, Batman!" screams Poison Ivy. "Or I will unleash the fullness of my wrath!"

"You preach freedom for plants," replies Batman, "but then you control them yourself for your own insane aims." He taps on the control panel, readying the freezer. "That's hypocritical."

Behind him, the shelves shudder, all the seeds vibrating, preparing to explode in a detonation of vegetation as Poison Ivy gathers her powers.

The control panel beeps. Batman flips the switch on the flash-freeze.

Poison Ivy's scream cuts off sharply and the seeds fall silent on the shelves.

Turn to page 78.

"Let's try modern technology," says Batman. "Show a satellite map of the Giordano Botanical Gardens hedge maze."

"Calculating," replies the communicator.

A map appears floating in Batman's vision through his goggles. He enlarges the maze, studying its twists and turns. His location appears as a blue dot.

He signals the computer to display the heat signature of other humans in the maze.

An infrared overlay appears, indicating a red dot near the exit. That's Poison Ivy ...

A sudden yank on his cowl snaps Batman's head. The map disappears. A branch from a hedge ripped off a bit of Batman's ear ... that contained his cowl's GPS antenna.

"Her plants must have picked up the signal," growls Batman. "I need to shield my satellite connection!"

If Batman decides to cut through the hedge walls, turn to page 67.

If he tries to find Poison Ivy using his memory of the map, turn to page 69.

With the flash-freeze compartment connected to a generator, Batman wheels the apparatus up to the surface. Police are waiting outside the conservatory, and they help him load the frozen Poison Ivy on to a truck.

Commissioner Gordon walks over from his car and shakes Batman's hand. "We won't defrost Poison Ivy until she's back in her cell," he promises. "Thank you for protecting the seed bank."

"It was my pleasure," says Batman. "It's too important a resource to fall under the control of someone with her own insane agenda."

"We're loaded and ready," a policewoman reports.

"Take her away," says Commissioner Gordon.

"I hope Arkham holds her for longer this time," says Batman.

THE END

To follow another path, turn to page 7.

"Don't forget to smell the lilacs," says Poison Ivy. "I find the scent ... intoxicating."

All around, the lilac bushes shake and shudder, the flowers quivering at Poison Ivy's command.

A dank purple mist rises out of the conical blossoms. The fumes drift around Batman, hanging heavy in the air.

The heady odour of the lilacs quickly intensifies. In seconds, the flowers' perfume becomes overwhelming. Batman gasps, feeling like he's choking on the floral stink.

It's only lilacs! The smell can't be that dangerous, can it?

While Batman is distracted by the stench, Ivy whirls at him, swinging her fists in a blur.

If Batman waves away the odour and fights Poison Ivy, turn to page 29.

If Batman puts on his oxygen mask first, turn to page 88.

Poison Ivy raises her hands. The peony blossoms quiver on their shrubs, and their smell intensifies. The scent isn't unpleasant, simply stronger.

"Is that supposed to make me back away?" asks Batman. "I like the smell of peonies."

Poison Ivy smiles.

That's when Batman realizes that the buzz of the bees has grown louder. The powerful perfume has called many more bees to the hedges.

The insects swoop around Poison Ivy, circling her in a loose cloud. Batman can feel their buzz rumbling in his chest.

He's got to stop her before she uses those stinging bees against him!

If Batman approaches Poison Ivy slowly, turn to page 68.
If he lunges at her, turn to page 92.

As silently as a panther stalking its prey, Batman slinks from pear tree to peach tree. He's careful not to step on any twigs or leaves.

He pulls himself into position behind a plum tree where he can see Poison Ivy, but she can't see him.

Poison Ivy listens to the orchard, as cautious as a deer. After a long moment of stillness and silence, she strides down the path towards the end of the orchard.

Batman creeps from plum tree to apple tree to pear tree, following her.

His foot lowers on to a stick. He freezes an instant before it can snap.

Whew, he thinks. *That was close.*

Then he safely slinks out of the orchard, and he spots Poison Ivy hurrying into the pine tree grove nearby.

Turn to page 61.

With Poison Ivy's unpredictable powers, Batman waits to see what she'll do before he makes a move.

"Cower before my flowers!" Poison Ivy exclaims. She flourishes her wrists and the crab apple petals begin to shake. The blooms begin to pop off the tree limbs like small pellets.

Batman holds up a hand, shielding his face from the onslaught of blossoms. "Calm down, Pamela!" he shouts. "This isn't necessary!"

Poison Ivy laughs. She pushes her hands out to her sides and the entire crab apple grove shoots its petals towards Batman. The petals slam Batman, sticking to his face, clogging his nose and mouth.

If Batman blindly tries to kick Poison Ivy to make her stop, turn to page 26.

If he shields himself under his cape, turn to page 60.

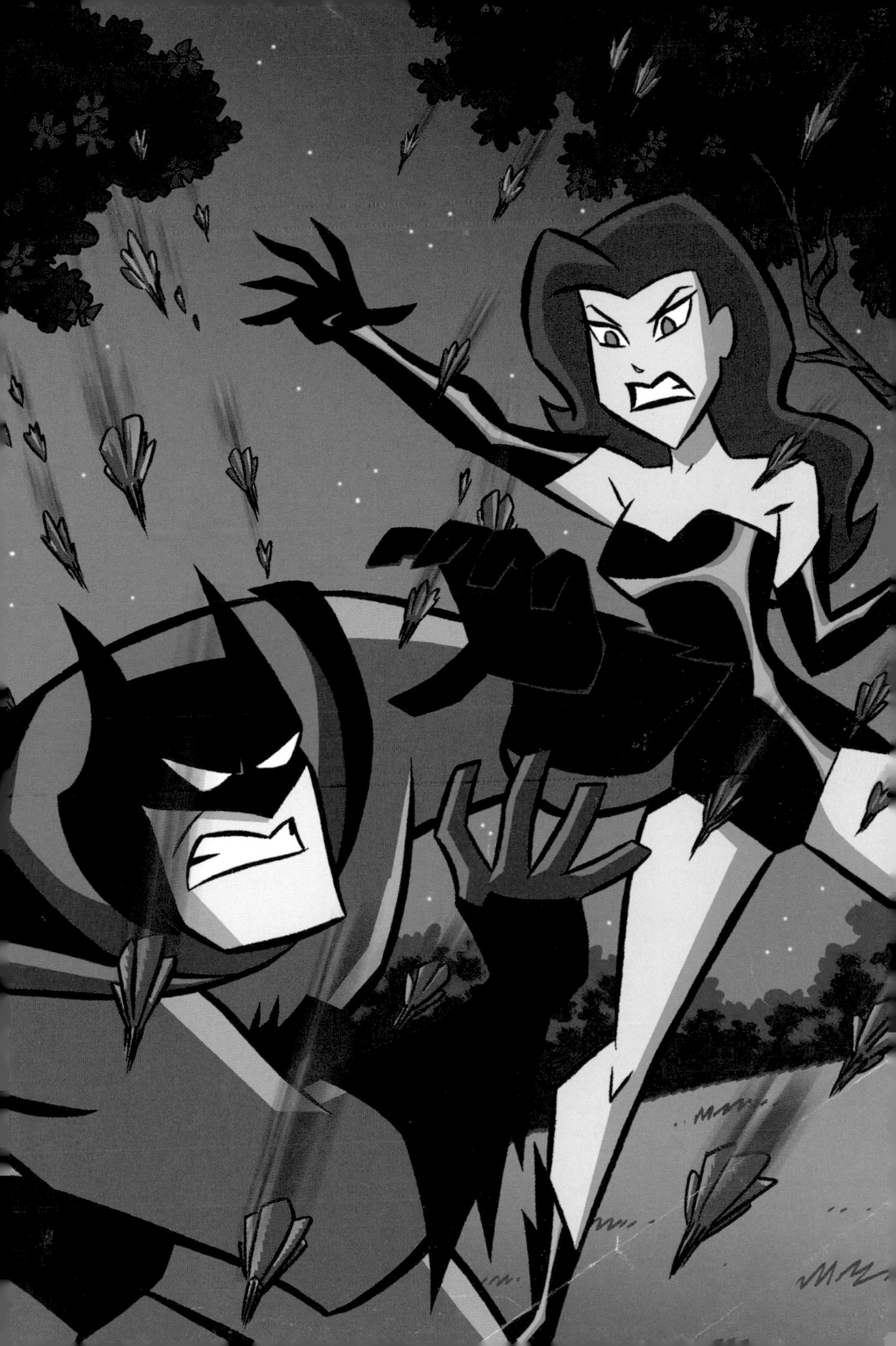

Poison Ivy slips into the hydrangea thicket, vanishing in the ferociously blooming flowers.

Batman chases her inside. Branches close around him, twigs tightening, snagging his cape. Blossoms shimmer purple to blue to pink to white and back again. The colours speed up, dazzling Batman. He feels dizzy and sick.

"Colour filter," Batman says. "Safe levels only." His goggles adjust.

He bashes through the hydrangea hedge, ripping his way out with the sharp batwings on his gauntlets.

He bursts free on to a grassy hill. Poison Ivy is nowhere in view.

The path splits in three directions. A sign states that the left branch leads to lilacs, the middle trail to peonies, and the route on the right to crab apples.

Which way should Batman search for Ivy?

If Batman searches the lilac bushes, turn to page 96.

If he checks the peony shrubs, turn to page 34.

If Batman investigates the crab apple grove, turn to page 54.

Batman ducks under the grasping strangler fig roots and rolls over to the garden hose coiled on the back of a fake boulder. The closest root grabs his foot and another snags his wrist.

He snaps one root with the boot on his free foot and slices through the other root with the sharp Batwings on his glove.

Before hundreds of roots can wrap around him, Batman raises the hose nozzle and sprays them full-blast with a stream of water.

They're smashed back against the banyan tree.

"My epiphytes!" cries Ivy. "No matter ... this whole conservatory is my arsenal!"

She clenches her fists. The banana trees behind her lean forward.

The ripe banana skins squeeze and shoot fruit at Batman like missiles.

If Batman throws his Batarangs at the bananas, turn to page 39.

If he avoids the bananas with acrobatic moves, turn to page 49.

Batman tries to break away and dart back along the path, but ferns rise up in front of him and block the way out.

The ferns grow quickly, expanding into a wild green monster.

"They may be monsters," Batman reminds himself, "but they're still just made up of ferns."

The fern lashes at Batman. The plant snaps at him with leafy teeth and then brandishes its spiked tail.

If Batman scrambles up a pine tree to escape, turn to page 43.

If he fights the fern, turn to page 59.

After Poison Ivy descends to the seed bank, Batman waits, counting to twenty. Then he scrambles towards the elevator.

Cacti fire their needles. Batman covers his face as he runs, and he hunches over in his cape when he reaches the doors. Spines stick into his back like a porcupine.

Batman ignores the jabs. He wrestles open the elevator doors and plunges into the shaft, swinging along the wires.

Landing hard on the elevator cab, Batman kicks out an access panel, then drops down into the box. It's open to the entrance of the seed bank.

Two uniformed guards lie unconscious in front of the unlocked vault. Their eyes swirl with flecks of toxic green.

"Poison Ivy used her mind control spores," says Batman.

Turn to page 25.

Batman flips backwards, away from Poison Ivy. He lands near the border of the lilac bushes, where the air is slightly clearer. While taking a moment to recuperate, Batman pulls his portable gas mask from his Utility Belt. He clips it over his mouth and nose, then heads back into the purple mist.

His head feels woozy again. "Computer," Batman says, "analyse airborne toxicity levels."

"The air is full of concentrated lilac fragrance," the computer reports, "but it is not poisonous."

"No wonder the gas mask doesn't filter it," growls Batman. "It's not toxic – just dizzying."

He's wasting too much time. Poison Ivy is getting away.

As he puts away his mask, Batman considers what else he could use from his Utility Belt.

If Batman takes out a matchstick and lights it, turn to page 18.

If he decides to power through the perfume without any tricks, turn to page 48.

Batman slides a sharp-edged Batarang out of his Utility Belt. Twisting, he slices at the sundew's tentacles, cutting those holding his shoulder.

He pulls his arm free, then leans down to chop the tentacles grabbing his leg.

That's when he feels a hard shove on his back.

Batman topples against the sundew, which wraps its tentacles around his body. Only Batman's face is free. He peers up to see Poison Ivy grinning at him.

"I couldn't let you cut up my beautiful sundew," she says. "Now you will be digested in its fatal hug." She runs off towards the seed bank.

Luckily, the sundew's digestive fluids don't affect Batman through his tough Batsuit, but he has to wait hours to be rescued from the plant by the police.

By the time he's freed, Poison Ivy is nowhere to be seen, and the seed bank is empty.

THE END

To follow another path, turn to page 7.

An old woman's cry comes from the central gazebo.

Batman rushes into the garden, yanking his cape free from thorns snagging him as he passes. Poison Ivy's mocking laughter echoes deep in the rows of roses.

Batman sees a senior couple sheltering in the gazebo. The old man bashes a vine with his cane, protecting his wife.

"Batman!" the woman cries. "Help us! We're here early every morning, but the roses never acted like this before!"

"Ivy makes them violent," explains Batman, leaping into the gazebo. "I'll protect you."

But there's not much to use to fight the blooming vines. A bare wooden trellis gives Batman an idea, but it might be smarter to stay sheltered in the gazebo.

If Batman hides with the old couple in the gazebo, turn to page 38.

If he uses the trellis to escape, turn to page 65.

Poison Ivy hurls a handful of tiny seeds at Batman. They start to sprout while still in mid-air, tangling in climbing stems, popping up lizard-shaped scarlet vegetables before they hit the ground.

Batman instantly recognizes the smell. "Peppers," he says.

"The spiciest peppers in the world," says Poison Ivy. "They're called ruby dragons. They're blazing hot, and they're coming for you."

The bulbous, bumpy red peppers crawl towards Batman on their wriggling stems.

Batman backs up. At any second, those vegetables may explode, spraying him with juice and seeds thousands of times hotter than a jalapeño!

"Eat one," says Poison Ivy, "and perhaps I'll turn myself in."

If Batman bites a chilli pepper, turn to page 31.
If he climbs the shelves to get away, turn to page 58.

Batman leaps forward, hoping to grab her before she can use the peonies to command the bees.

But before he gets close, Poison Ivy tilts her head, and the peonies around him spurt pollen on his face. He has to stop to sneeze and wipe his goggles.

"*Gesundheit,*" says Poison Ivy, smirking.

"Thank you," replies Batman.

The bees stop circling her. They zoom towards Batman, and he tries not to flinch as they swoop at his head.

He freezes as the bees gather on his chin and cheeks. In seconds, they've formed a thick, buzzing, crawly beard hanging down to his chest.

The feeling of hundreds of tiny legs and flickering antennae and fuzzy bee bodies creeping on his face itches like crazy.

If Batman slaps the bees crawling on his face, turn to page 47.
If he calmly approaches Poison Ivy, turn to page 68.

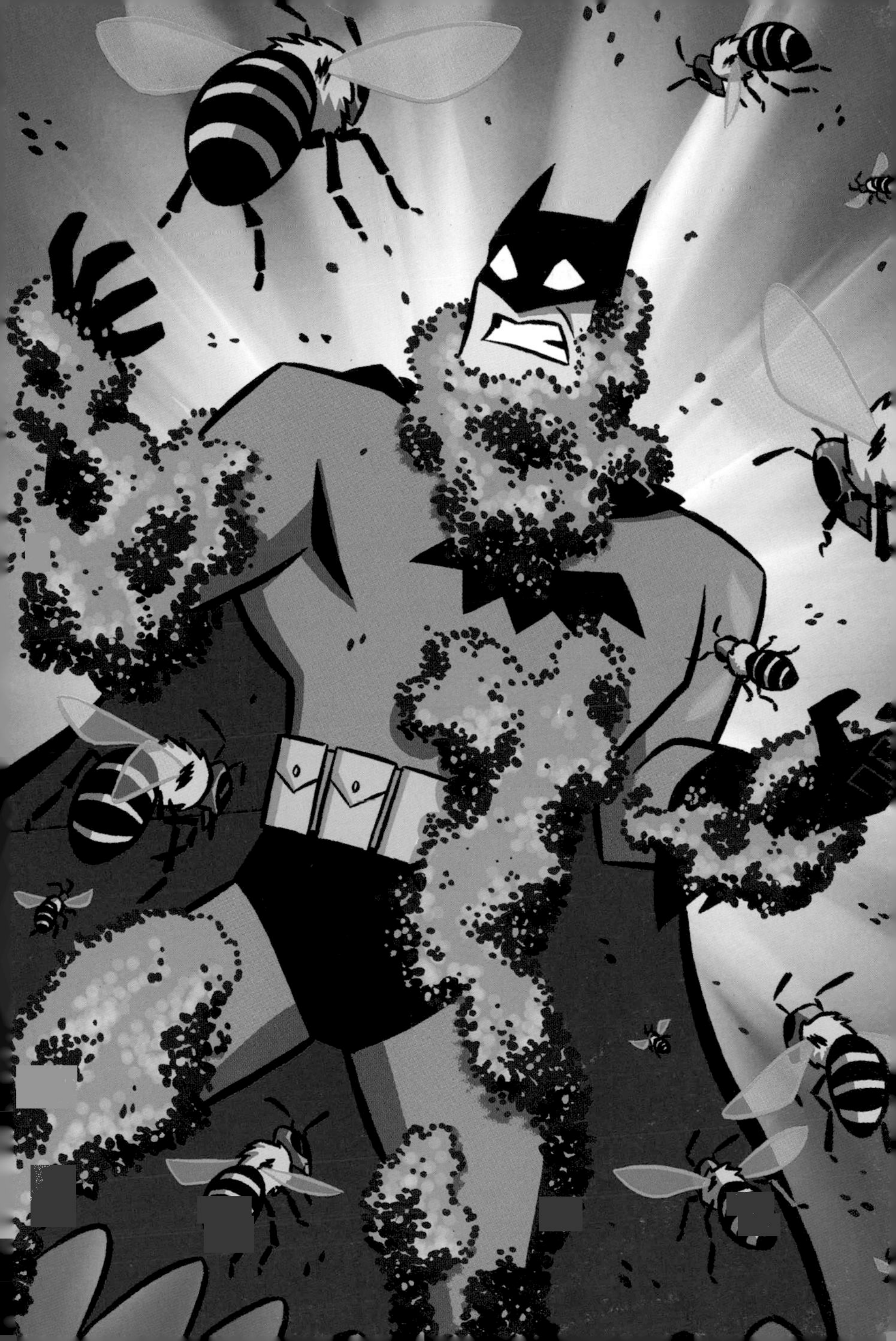

Poison Ivy's eyes blaze. The cucumber and tomato vines explode into a wild snarl.

Before Batman can move, the vines twine up his legs, grabbing his arms, tangling him up until he can't move at all.

"That will hold you long enough," says Poison Ivy. "Kids, don't try to free Batman, or the vines will grab you, too!"

Poison Ivy casually saunters out of the vegetable garden towards the seed bank.

She robs the botanical garden while Batman struggles uselessly in the vines.

Worst of all, all the young students watch Batman's defeat with wide, disappointed eyes.

THE END

To follow another path, turn to page 7.

With the nuclear chilli in his face, Batman realizes that it's best to talk to Poison Ivy. "Wait," he says. "This vault protects the seeds in case of a catastrophe. Why don't you support that, Pamela?"

"My name is Poison Ivy," she replies. "Of course you wouldn't understand."

"Please explain," says Batman. "I'm interested in hearing your reasons. Is it because you're afraid for the safety of the seeds in the bank?"

"No!" cries Poison Ivy. "It's insane that humans think plants need protection. From whom? From humans! If people treated Mother Nature with the respect she deserves, there would be no need for a seed bank, no need to collect and label and control the plants' hopes for the future!"

"I completely agree," says Batman.

Turn to page 57.

Batman catches a glimpse of Ivy's red hair before she disappears behind the fat lilac bushes. He runs towards her, hopping over an ankle-high white picket fence circling the hill.

The bushes are dense with cone-shaped lavender blooms. Each bush is a foot taller than Batman. He gets a strong whiff of the powerful lilac fragrance as he charges towards the spot where he last saw Poison Ivy.

A shapely green leg jams out from behind a bush, tripping Batman.

Batman ducks forward and rolls between two shrubs. He springs up again, whirling around to face his enemy.

Poison Ivy smiles.

Turn to page 79.

After the bee stings him, Batman grits his teeth. His chin throbs with pain, but he holds still as Poison Ivy turns and strides out of the peony hedges. She disappears around the curve of the hill.

After she leaves, the bees buzz around Batman for a few more moments. Without Poison Ivy's powers affecting the peony perfume, the smell fades into the breeze.

The bees lose interest in Batman and return to their business collecting pollen.

As soon as he's free of bees, Batman takes off running, chasing after Poison Ivy.

He sees her down at the base of the hill, slipping through the ornate iron gate that leads into the rose garden.

Turn to page 40.

Using the tractor to fight Poison Ivy's vast vegetables seems like the best bet, but the farm vehicle is all the way on the other side of the garden. In between are the humongous cucumbers, the celery forest and large globular heads of lettuce flapping their leaves menacingly.

The grotesquely plump tomatoes wiggle, ready to fall and crush the students.

"Batman, help us!" the teacher cries.

Batman focuses on the tractor. He has to move now.

"You're thinking about that tractor," says Ivy. "My vines will grab you before you get close."

How can Batman get past the creeping vines?

If he swings on a giant celery stalk, turn to page 50.
If he vaults over a gargantuan cucumber, turn to page 94.

Batman shoves the saguaro to the floor, then swirls his cape around himself from his nose down to the ground.

He can feel the needles hit. So many spines smack him at once that he stumbles backward. His heel squashes a juicy succulent plant, and he slips. Batman's back slams against a cork bulletin board.

"Volley!" Poison Ivy shrieks. "Silhouette him!"

The cacti launch needles again, twice as many as before. This time, the needles don't hit Batman's body — they surround him in an outline, pinning his cape to the cork.

Batman wriggles, but he's stuck tight.

"You lose, Batman," says Poison Ivy. "Sorry to be so sharp, but you get the point."

Then she robs the seed bank.

THE END

To follow another path, turn to page 7.

Batman leaps forward, hurling himself at Poison Ivy.

She sidesteps, twists sideways, and slams her clasped fists on Batman's back.

Surprised, Batman stumbles, but then catches himself, rolling forward and landing in a ready squat. He forgot how agile and strong Ivy is. No way will he underestimate her again.

He flips on to his hands, launching at her feet-first.

Before Batman reaches Ivy, she clenches her fist and a bristly flowering crab apple limb stretches in front of her, blocking his attack. The branches shove him back, deeper into the grove.

Batman spits out a pink petal as the limb retreats. "You're crabby today," he says.

"Get out of my way," replies Poison Ivy.

Again she raises her hands, and her eyes glow.

If Batman crouches defensively before acting, turn to page 82.

If he tries a roundhouse kick to Ivy's head, turn to page 26.

"I never realized how similar farming is to slavery," says Batman, although he can't believe he keeps a straight face.

"Good," says Poison Ivy, smiling. "You see the light."

"Yes," says Batman. "You make a persuasive case for freeing plants." He sees the open flash-freeze apparatus behind her, leaking frosty air. The ruby dragon pepper dangles in front of his eyes, pulling his focus back to the dangerous chilli. "If we both leave the seed bank now, we can discuss the next step on our mission of plant mercy."

"I could use your help," says Poison Ivy. "The authorities will listen to you."

"That's right," says Batman. "So let's leave the seed bank and get started on freedom."

"Yes," says Poison Ivy. "Let's."

If Batman trusts Poison Ivy, turn to page 66.
If he pushes her into the flash-freeze compartment, turn to page 76.

"If you're not scared," replies Poison Ivy, "you must be stupid."

Batman doesn't bother to reply. He crouches, ready for whatever horrible thing Poison Ivy will throw at him.

Poison Ivy blows a kiss at a saguaro cactus beside her. The spiny plant is nine feet tall and has two upraised arms like a crook surrendering to police.

Lowering its arms in a boxer's stance, the cactus punches the air.

"Talk about stupid," Batman says, shaking his head in dismay.

The saguaro throws a sharp right jab at Batman's face.

If Batman runs away from the boxing cactus, turn to page 41.
If he spars with the saguaro, turn to page 71.

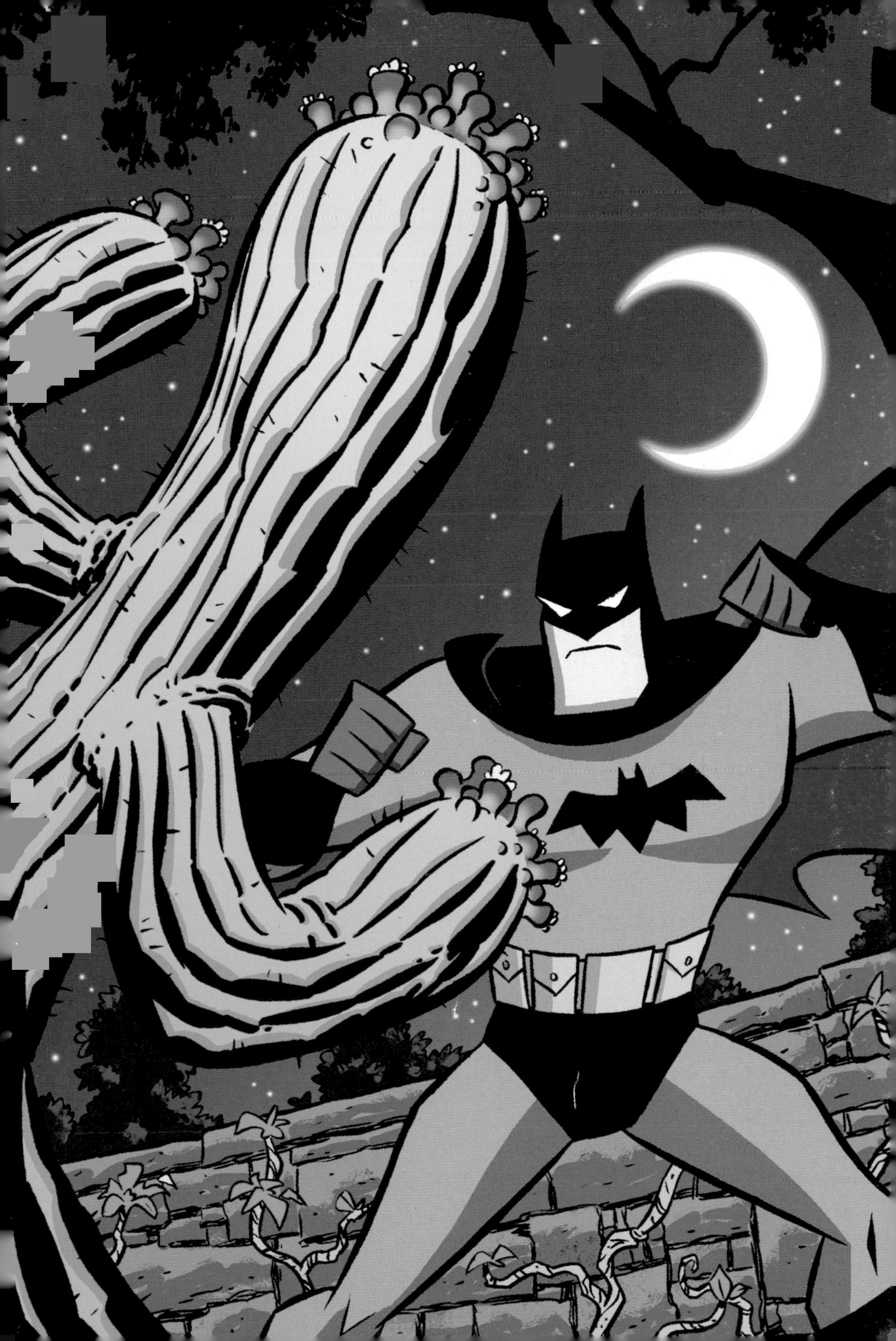

Batman follows Poison Ivy into an area surrounded by a chicken-wire fence. Inside are rows of low planting boxes filled with soil and lined with growing vegetables. Batman hurries around a tractor, running along an aisle between carrots, celery, lettuce, tomatoes and cucumbers.

Over by a shed, a dozen schoolchildren scream, sitting up in sleeping bags. Batman veers in that direction.

"You camped out here?" Batman asks their teacher.

"Yes," she explains, "to teach these city students about farm life!"

The kids shriek and point behind Batman.

Poison Ivy stands between the garden rows, her arms outstretched, her eyes glowing green. The plants wriggle and squirm, soil churning. The vegetables swell, growing to enormous size.

"I don't like farm life!" a girl sobs.

Turn to page 20.

As Batman reaches the end of the glass tunnel, Ivy has already entered the carnivorous plant room. Batman bursts in after her.

The smaller greenhouse environment is as hot, sunny, and humid as the jungle room, but the smell is totally different. The soil is dark, wet peat bog, and it stinks like a swamp. Flies and gnats buzz above beds of tall pitcher plants, low hummocks of Venus flytrap plants, and mounds of dainty, glistening sundews.

Poison Ivy doesn't waste any time with threats. The room is full of nothing but threats.

Her eyes glow toxic green, and she concentrates all her powers on a Venus flytrap between her and Batman.

Batman crouches down, on high alert. That plant eats meat!

Turn to page 72.

POISON IVY

Real Name:
Pamela Isley

Occupation:
Botanist, criminal

Base:
Gotham City

Height:
1.67 m (5 ft. 6 in.)

Weight:
50 kg (110 lbs.)

Eyes:
Green

Hair:
Chestnut

Pamela Isley was born with immunities to plant toxins and poisons. Her love of plants began to grow like a weed at an early age. She eventually became a botanist, or plant scientist. Through reckless experimentation with various flora, Pamela Isley's skin itself has become poisonous. Her venomous lips and plant weapons present a real problem for crime fighters. But Ivy's most dangerous quality is her extreme love of nature – she cares more about the smallest seed than any human.

* Poison Ivy was once engaged to Gotham City's District Attorney, Harvey Dent, who eventually became the super-villain Two-Face! Their relationship ended when Dent built a prison on a field of wildflowers.

* Poison Ivy emits toxic fragrances that can be harmful to humans. Whenever she is locked up in Arkham Asylum, a wall of plexiglass must separate her from the guards to ensure their safety.

* Ivy may love her plant creations, but that love hasn't always been returned. A man-eating plant of her own design became self-aware, or sentient. The thing called itself Harvest and turned on Ivy.

* Ivy's connection to plants is so strong that she can control them by thought alone.

AUTHOR

J.E. Bright is the author of many novels, novelizations, and novelty books for children and young adults. He lives in a sunny apartment in the Washington Heights neighbourhood of Manhattan, USA, with his difficult but soft cat, Mabel, and his sweet kitten, Bernard.

ILLUSTRATOR

Ethen Beaver is a professional comic book artist from Modesto, California, USA. His best-known works for DC Comics include Justice League Unlimited and Legion of Superheroes in the 31st Century. He has also illustrated for other top publishers, including Marvel, Dark Horse and Abrams.

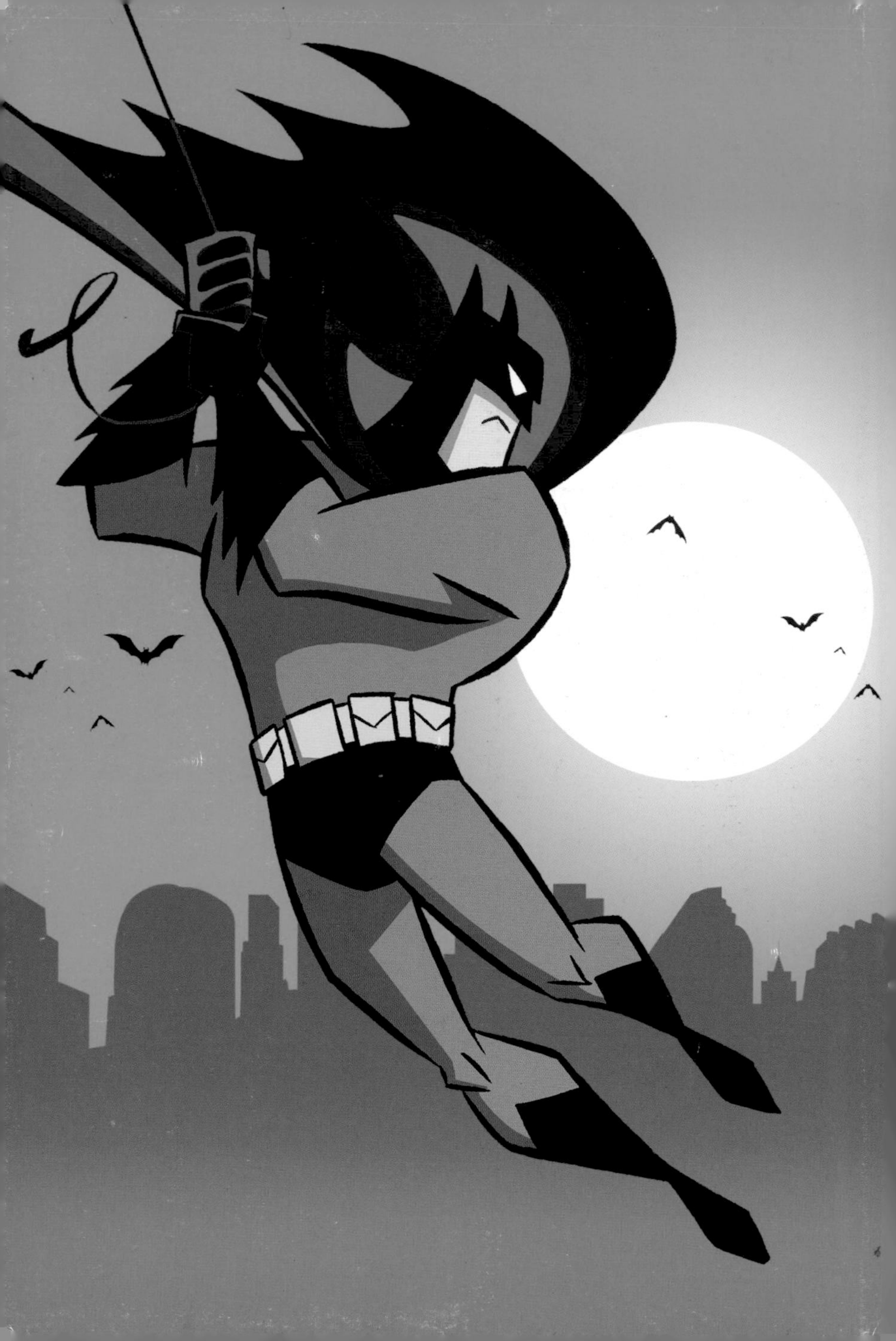

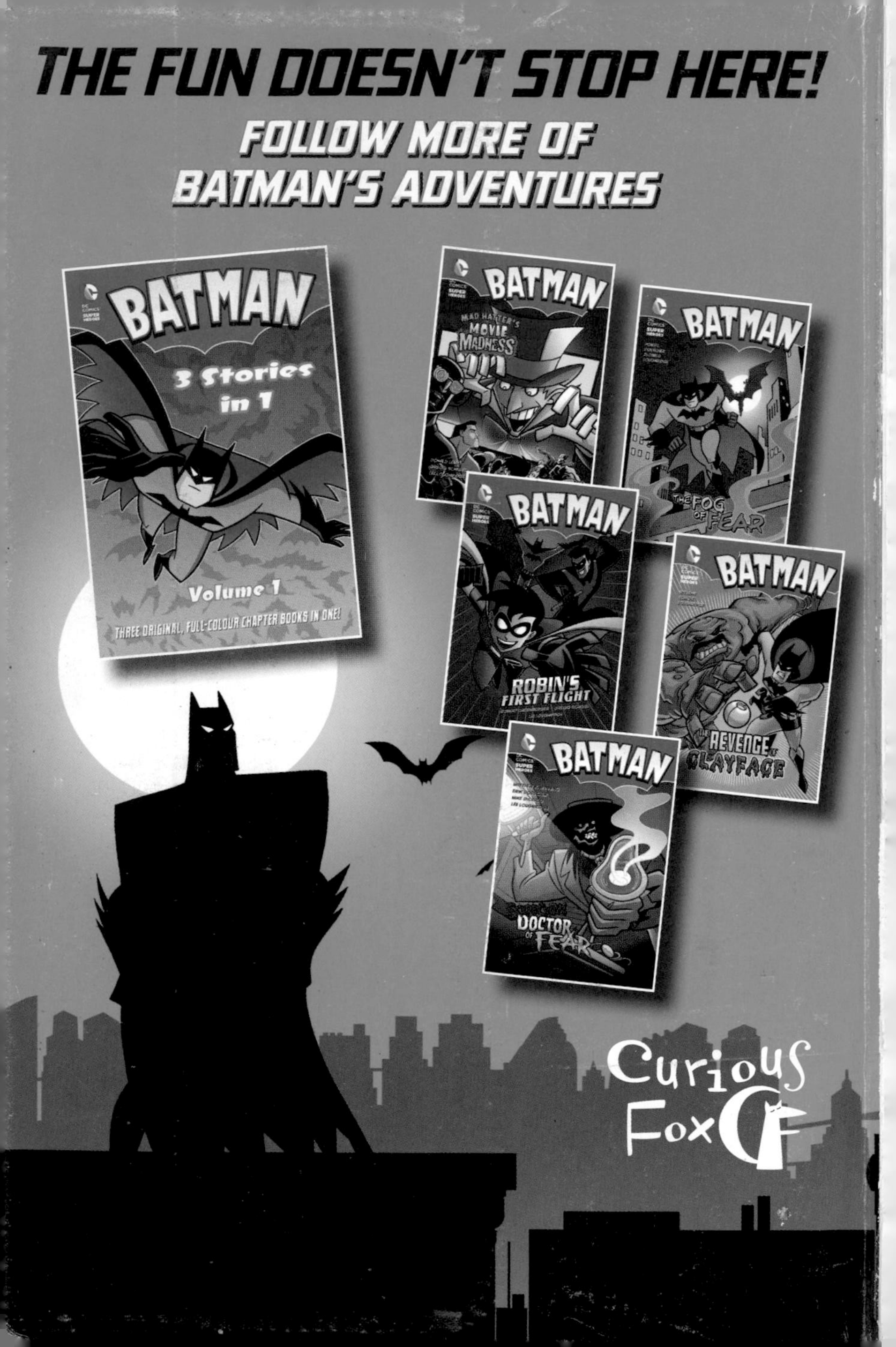
THE FUN DOESN'T STOP HERE!
FOLLOW MORE OF BATMAN'S ADVENTURES
BATMAN
3 Stories in 1
Volume 1
THREE ORIGINAL, FULL-COLOUR CHAPTER BOOKS IN ONE!
BATMAN
MAD HATTER'S MOVIE MADNESS
BATMAN
THE FOG OF FEAR
BATMAN
ROBIN'S FIRST FLIGHT
BATMAN
REVENGE OF CLAYFACE
BATMAN
DOCTOR OF FEAR
Curious Fox